Psychic Kim Stride in the Mozart Mystery

Joanne L. Napoli

Psychic Detective Kim Stride in the Mozart Mystery

Contents

DEDICATION

This novel is dedicated to my parents,
John and Lillyan Napoli, who introduced me to
classical music at an early age, and first took me to
Europe, starting my life-long love for European
countries, with their various histories, cultures and
languages.

ACKNOWLEDGMENTS

I am deeply indebted to Dr. Vernon Katz for introducing me to ancient Indian scriptures and understanding their meanings, particularly *The Upanishads* which I refer to in this book.

My dear friend, Doris Kretz, introduced me to the Swiss Alps and other parts of Switzerland which form a part of my story.

In addition, I would like to thank all those who helped me with the computer set-up and proof editing of this second edition of my book, especially Sandri Kim, George Oberlander and Jessica Fay. I also valued the feedback from members of the English Hour Book Club community at Duke University International House in preparing this edition.

Many thanks to Angélique Droesseart for creating the cover art for this edition. Her photo artwork perfectly expresses the delight and playfulness I envisioned in writing this novel.

I also thank my son, David Altman, who encouraged me to reprint my book.

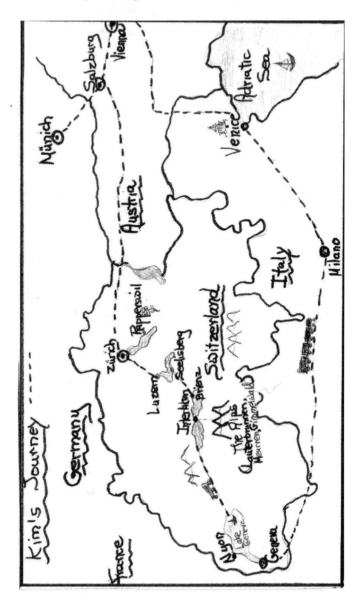

CHAPTER ONE: A FIERY VISION

When 13-year-old Kimberly woke up that morning, she didn't know where she was, or even who she was. She couldn't even remember what century she was living in because she had a dream, or rather a nightmare. A terrified child was screaming as she fell through fiery gusts of air with a strange bundle of parchment papers stuffed into her jacket! And now, it was all a blank.

This had never happened to Kim before. Who could that child be? Resisting this pull towards what felt like a void inside her, she opened her eyes and looked up at the ceiling and the window frame. Slowly, ever so slowly, it was coming back to her. She was named Kimberly Stride, Professor Daniel Stride's only child. She and her father lived alone in an old wood frame house a block away from the University where he was a music professor, a specialist in Mozart's music.

The tree-lined lane where their Victorian house sat had been her home ever since she could remember, even before her mother had died when she was five, leaving them alone to fend for themselves. Her dad never talked much about how her mother died. It was too painful for him. Kim's only friend was Sam Berlow, who lived two houses away, and whose mother taught Asian Studies.

It was still very early in the morning, and Kim

began to hear the sweet sounds of birds in the huge oak tree outside her window. Since it was summer, she didn't have to get up for school. She had just finished her first year at Meadow Gardens Middle School, and the change was quite a shock for her. She didn't feel that she fit in anywhere at her new school, certainly not with the snobby cliques or with the nerds. Suddenly, a pebble thudded on the window, followed by a bird-like whistle. "It must be Sam," she thought as she stumbled out of bed, still a little dizzy from her out-of-time experience.

If it weren't for Sam, she would have felt even more out of place. She found it easy to tell him about her experiences and he actually believed her. Kim liked Sam a lot because he could be funny and since his mother was also at the University, they could talk to each other about the strange ways of professors. Sam was hooked on video games, but Kim preferred to spend more time outside, going for walks and seeing if she could identify some of the birds that lived in the area. She also liked to sit next to the duck pond by herself sometimes, gazing at the new ducklings that were just beginning to swim along with their mother. They followed her in an orderly row while the male duck, stretching his green-gold neck, kept a watchful eye.

"Hey, Kim," Sam called out, as she opened the window. "Want to come over to my house? My Mom's still asleep and we can play the cool new video game I just got – Well of Evil. It's got nine levels."

"I'll be down in a minute, Sam," she said.

Sam was expectantly waiting for Kimberly outside on the porch, ready for action, as always. She admired his love of adventure. When he got an idea in his head, nothing could stop him. Instead, Kim was always second-guessing the "what-ifs" of a situation and doubting that she could do it.

"So, do you want to see the new video game?" he asked.

"Let's take a walk first," she suggested. It was too nice a day to be wasted indoors. Besides, Sam, Kim, and her father would be leaving soon for their trip to Salzburg, Austria. Just a month ago, Kim's father had sat the two of them down in the Stride's living room and said that he had plans for them this summer:

"My department just gave me a travel grant to Salzburg to authenticate a music manuscript supposedly written by Mozart: a cello concerto!"

He sounded very excited. Kim learned enough about Mozart to know that there was no record of his ever having written a cello concerto.

"I found out about it from an old friend, Karl Hess. I studied at the Mozarteum in Salzburg with him," said her dad. "He works for an old book dealer, a man named Hauser. As soon as I got his note, I immediately went to the University and they acted fast; if it gets widely known that the manuscript exists, we might lose a chance to take a first crack at it."

Kim could tell that this meant a lot to her father. He'd always been telling her how important it was for someone in his field to a make a "musical discovery."

"I have enough money from the grant to stay a month, and if the manuscript is authentic, then the University will arrange to have me buy it, especially if it's in Mozart's own handwriting!" Professor Stride added. "Then, it will be really valuable! Luckily, a wealthy donor offered a great deal of money to buy it. But, I thought that instead of having you stay with the Berlows while I was gone, you could come with me," he said to Kim.

Kim's face brightened; this was going to be a real adventure!

"You can come with us, too," he added, when he saw the look of disappointment on Sam's face. "I already asked your mother; she said it was okay with her."

Sam smiled broadly, but when he turned to Kim, he looked a little embarrassed. He liked her as a good friend, but he didn't want to be that obvious about it. In the past month after this announcement, Professor Stride quickly made the arrangements for plane tickets, passports and all of the other details. In only a few days, they'd be on their way.

As the two friends walked along the road, they were passing the house where the neighbor's white dog would run and bark viciously at them, his cute little face masking his ferocious growl. Although Sam was scared of the dog, Kim enjoyed moments like these because it gave her a chance to try making things happen through her imagination. Once again, like numerous times before this, she concentrated all her energy from the space between her eyes to the space between the dog's eyes. Along this pathway, she sent love and light to this little dog. In response, the dog stopped barking and looked confused, just letting out a little yelp. Then he just stood there acting like he was dizzy while they quietly walked by.

"I can't understand how you do that," said Sam.

"It's so easy," replied Kim. "I just look at him and send him love."

"If it's so easy, then why can't I do it?"

"I don't know. Maybe it just takes practice."

Sam sensed that Kim had some special gift, more than he could understand. As much as he tried, he felt like he was lagging behind as she demonstrated such amazing abilities in their ordinary lives. He remembered how she broke up a fight between two girls at school by just watching them and sending out thoughts of friendship between them.

"Sam, I have to tell you something weird that happened to me this morning, as I was waking up," said Kim.

"I'm all ears, Kim."

"I just lost all sense of who or where I was. I felt like I didn't even know which century I was in."

"No kidding! I just heard about something like that," said Sam. "My mom was talking about an Indian scripture called *The Upanishads*. She said that there is a state of awareness which is beyond time and place," said Sam. Hearing these words, Kim felt relieved. She was beginning to think that something strange and beyond her control was happening to her.

"You have no idea how much you just helped me, Sam! I thought that maybe I was losing my mind. Now you tell me that I am not as weird as I thought."

"Maybe my mom can tell you more about this," said Sam.

"Sure, I would be happy to talk with her," said Kim, just a little nervous.

That evening, Kim went over to Sam's house to find out about this "timeless" experience from Sam's mom. Entering the hallway, Mrs. Berlow, a fit and attractive woman with curly brown hair, welcomed Kim.

I am so pleased to meet you, Kim. Sam has told me about your latest experience."

"I'm pleased to meet you, too, Mrs. Berlow," Kim responded.

"Please come and sit down," said Sam's mom. "I would like to hear all about your experience. You know, I have been studying and teaching the ancient Indian scriptures for twenty years, but I never actually experienced those states of awareness that were mentioned in the text."

"Well, I'm not so sure that what I experienced is all that special," answered Kim. Then, she began to describe the timeless, placeless feelings she'd been having.

"Oh, yes," answered Mrs. Berlow. "Those are most definitely the ways they are described in *The Upanishads*. Once you know what is happening, it can be very blissful. You are actually a living example that those scriptures are valid and real. I am really quite surprised and even envious that someone as young as you has already had them."

"Thank you. I don't quite know what to say," said Kim, very flustered.

"Don't worry. I would love to be your guide along the way. Whenever you have questions about your experiences, please feel free to ask me anything. I will do what I can to give you the actual written text to authenticate them. In the meantime, here is a copy of *The Upanishads* for you to keep. You might want to read it whenever you get a chance."

Mrs. Berlow handed the paperback copy to her. It had a picture of a weird man dancing on it, with a few more arms than normal coming out of his body.

"Who is that?" asked Kim.

"That's from a statue of Shiva who dances in that state of blissful awareness. You will learn more about these representations of the Divine as you get into Indian mythology," answered Mrs. Berlow.

Kim felt so relieved that she could relax and enjoy these experiences, knowing that someone wise had written about them and that they were real. Not quite "normal," but also not so weird. Of course, this still didn't explain her vision of the terrified child and the fiery air. And what were those parchment papers stuffed in that little girl's clothes? None of that made any sense, at least not yet. Although Kim wanted to forget about that vision, she still couldn't help feeling curious about it. What did it mean?

CHAPTER TWO: SALZBURG REVISITED

The day had arrived for their trip to Europe. Kim and Sam were very excited about traveling to another continent and seeing a much older world as described in their history books. Lately, they were pouring over maps and reading about Austria and life in the seventeenth century. What struck Kim as really strange was that some of the clothes described in the books reminded her of the child in her dream. Could she possibly have had a vision dating back to those times? This journey to Europe might help her understand her dream.

Now they were at the airport in New York, ready to get a flight to Munich, Germany, the closest transatlantic destination to Salzburg, Austria. All around them, they heard people speaking in other languages, mostly German. Their excitement grew as they waited for their flight.

"Hey, Kim, did you hear that? Those people must come from Europe. I can't understand them at all. Can you, Professor Stride?" asked Sam, looking up at Stride who was sitting next to him and reading a newspaper.

"Oh, yes, Sam. After all, I studied in Salzburg and had to learn German in order to understand my teachers. Mostly everyone knew German."

"Dad, don't you feel excited to go back there again?" asked Kim.

"Sure. It's not like my first time, you know. But I do feel a little excited to return there."

Then, they heard the announcement to board their flight. Kim felt butterflies in her stomach as she followed her father on the ramp leading to the plane. As they were finding their seats, Sam followed close behind, saying "Look how far we are from the ground." Kim looked out the small window and realized how big this jumbo jet really was. She felt a little queasy as she slid into her small seat.

After an eight-hour ride across the Atlantic Ocean, the plane landed in Munich. They switched to a train connecting to Salzburg. As they were crossing the border into Austria, Kim was still groggy from having lost a night's sleep by crossing time zones backwards. She looked out the train window to see mountains off in the distance and chalets with red streaming flowers trailing from balconies. *"It's just like the picture books of Germany in "Grimm's Fairy Tales,"* she thought. Sam was half asleep, barely able to keep his eyes open, yet forcing himself to stay awake to see this whole new world he had always been dreaming about in history books. Professor Stride had seen this all before when he studied piano and music history at the Mozarteum Conservatory in Salzburg, so he just closed his eyes, the passports and tickets safely tucked away in his inside pocket.

After a few hours, they finally arrived at the Salzburg train station. Lugging their bags, they took the bus into the heart of the old city. When they arrived by the side of the Salzach River, Kim couldn't believe how lovely it all looked. The old houses were painted all sorts of pastel colors and looked like they were leaning on one another, huddling together from the forces of nature and time.

The fast-moving river flowed between the two sides of the city, connected with bridges. It was summer and the international musical festival was going on, so people from all over the world thronged the streets.

"Dad, I can't believe how lucky you were to study here for two whole years. This is like being in a fantasy land," said Kim, enchanted with the scene.

"Oh, yes, it was really terrific to live here and be a music student. In fact, we will stay in a little chalet near the international student house where I lived, just outside the city," he replied.

"Do you mean that students lived there from all different countries? How did you speak to each other?" asked Sam.

"Well, we learned each other's languages—mainly German, English and French—and of course, we spoke the universal language: music," said Stride.

The bus wound its way along the river into the countryside and they got off beside a small chalet where they rented rooms for a month. A sweet-looking woman named Frau Huber and her blond daughter, Heidi, who looked about Kim's age, greeted them at the door.

"Now, I know that I'm in a fantasy, Sam, when a girl's name is Heidi, like in the novel I used to read," said Kim, "I hope that we get to know her a little while we're here."

After a good night's sleep in their small rooms, under summer weight fluffy blankets, they all met on the flower-decked balcony to have breakfast, or "Frühstuck," as it was called in Austria. They ate freshly baked "Semmeln" rolls with homemade jam, and coffee with milk which Heidi brought in on a tray. Stride invited her to sit down and talk with them.

"How wonderful it must be to live here surrounded by mountains," Sam said to Heidi, curious to see how

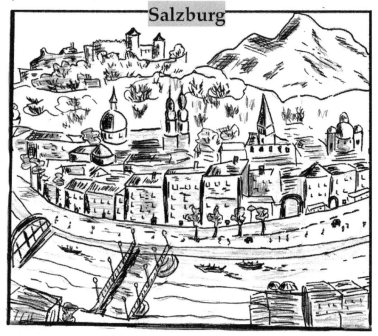

Salzburg

well she spoke English.

"I am used to it, so it seems very normal to me," she answered. "Instead, I dream of traveling to America, where you live."

"But to us, America isn't so special, since we're used to it," answered Kim.

"You speak English quite well, Heidi," said Sam. "Where did you learn it?"

"We learn English in school when we are very young," said Heidi. "And I always speak to the Americans who come to stay in our chalet."

Kim liked Heidi enormously. She was so natural with her long blond braids and blue eyes. Sam was taking a liking to her also. This was pretty obvious by the way he listened intently to every word she spoke.

After finishing breakfast, the adventurers were ready to explore. Before doing the business of locating and viewing the Mozart manuscript, Stride decided to show the children around the area. First, they went to town to see the Mozarteum where he had studied. As they walked up the imposing steps to the gray stone building, they could hear music coming from everywhere as students were either practicing or taking lessons on all sorts of instruments. It was a cacophony of sound all jumbled up, until they entered the concert "Saal" which was just filling up with people coming to hear a piano competition about to start.

"We won't stay here today, since there is so much I want to show you," said Stride.

As they were leaving, Kim suddenly heard a cello playing a haunting melody.

"Dad, did you hear that cello playing?"

"What cello, Kim? I don't hear anything."

"Oh never mind; it must be my imagination." Still, Kim was wondering why she could hear it so clearly and her dad couldn't. She wondered if this was another of those special moments from the past.

Next, they went to the center of town where Mozart's house had been kept intact, near a street called the Getreidegasse. From the outside, it looked just like one of the other buildings with rows of windows, except it was painted yellow. Maybe in the days before electricity, they needed so many windows for daylight, thought Kim. Since there was a long line of people waiting to enter, they decided to come back later when it was less crowded. As they walked along the cobble-stoned medieval street, Kim noticed that the shop signs were very old and ornate: "Look, Dad, the signs have such interesting carvings and metal work on them."

"Yes," said Stride, "Each merchant took special

care to produce beautiful signs with pictures or icons to display their wares. In fact, the name of the street means 'grain street' because that's what they sold a lot of here."

Along the way, they noticed little stone archway galleries, some of them leading into courtyards where there were tables and chairs surrounded by potted plants and trees. They followed these endless mazes in and around the old town and sometimes landed up at old churches or outdoor restaurants. It was an adventure just to walk around without any destination in mind.

"There's one thing I don't understand," said Sam. "How can a manuscript get lost for almost 200 years?

"You wouldn't know this," said Stride, "but the first Haydn cello concerto was also 'lost' for at least that amount of time when it was discovered in the 1960s. Sometimes these old manuscripts have been locked away somewhere until someone looks at them more closely and discovers a treasure."

"Dad, where is the location of the manuscript you were sent here to see?'

"We're almost there, Kim," said Stride. "Hauser's music shop lies along this street. We can see a little more of the town first or we can go there now."

"Oh, yes, Dad, let's go now," said Kim. "I can't wait to get inside one of these stores."

They located the music store that was brimming with old music books and sheet music on crowded shelves. It smelled musty from the old paper. Stride walked over to a balding man in a dark brown suit. He immediately recognized him as his old friend, Karl Hess.

"Karl!" Stride said. "It's been a long time, hasn't it?"

The man looked up from the manuscript he'd

been reading, smiled broadly, and gave Stride an embrace.

"Daniel," he said. "So good to see you; and these must be your children?" he asked, looking at Kim and Sam.

"This is my daughter, Kim," said Stride. Kim offered her hand which Hess shook warmly. And then Stride introduced Sam.

"We must have a beer together soon," said Hess enthusiastically. "But right now, I have some disappointing news for you," he added, his tone changing abruptly. "But I'd best let Herr Hauser tell you."

He then took them into an inner room where an old man with thick glasses sat at a table, his head held between his hands until he heard them enter.

"I am glad to meet you Professor Stride. However, I have some bad news for you," he said. "The valuable manuscript you were expecting to see today has apparently been stolen. When I opened the vault this morning, it was missing. I looked everywhere, just in case it was accidentally misplaced, but still I could not find it. Please excuse me. I am very overwrought."

"But who else knew about this manuscript?" asked Stride.

"Only a select few of the best-known music and book dealers in the world," replied Hauser. "I will continue to search for it and will let you know if I can locate it. Please give me a telephone number where I can reach you. I don't want to inform the authorities just yet until I have a proper chance to conduct a meticulous search of the shop."

When they were about to walk out, Hess stopped Stride with a nod.

"I was very surprised and shocked by this unexpected news, too, Daniel," he said. "But we must get together later and talk. Perhaps I might be able to help you in this matter."

The three left the store, totally perplexed by the loss of the manuscript. Stride didn't know what to do since he had only been given instructions to examine and authenticate the manuscript and to buy it with the money he was authorized to offer.

Then Kim found herself saying, "Don't worry, Dad. It will show up. I'm sure of it."

"How can you be so sure?" asked Sam, as Stride looked at her curiously.

"I don't know what made me say that, but somehow I know that we will find it," she replied. She even amazed herself because she never usually felt sure of anything in her life.

The next afternoon, since they had not yet heard from Hauser, Stride decided to rent bicycles for Kim and Sam. They were going with Heidi to explore the meadow paths around the student house while he anxiously waited for the call from Hauser. Kim remembered seeing the back of the Frohnburg student house in "The Sound of Music" when the Trapp family was pushing the car out of the courtyard to escape the Nazis. The three then bicycled down Hellbrunner Alleé, a tree-lined dirt road where the trees gracefully formed a green archway over their heads.

As they cycled down the Alleé, towards the riding stables and the wilderness zoo where animals were fenced in their natural habitat, Kim had a strong sensation of having done this before. She felt as if she had been in this place in another time, hundreds of years ago. In fact, she felt as if she were wearing other clothes and riding on a horse instead of a bicycle. She knew every tree, every house and every stream along the way. It was a strange feeling, but she accepted it as part of what was said in *The Upanishads. After all, if it's possible to be in a timeless zone, it's also possible to dip into any particular time along the way,* she thought.

When they returned, one look at Stride's anxious face told her that there had been no news about the manuscript. Stride pretended that he wasn't worried, but the meal they had at a local restaurant that evening was very somber. They all just picked at their food.

That night, while Kim was drifting off to sleep, listening to the small birds trilling their evening songs, she began to see a scene unfolding before her eyes. *She was dressed in something very strange – a long old-fashioned dress with billowy, lace sleeves. She was standing by an old style piano, one that looked almost like the old harpsichord in the music department where her dad taught. But she was also near someone who was sitting at the piano feverishly writing down notes on parchment. She could actually see him from the side, and the profile looked like someone she knew.*

He was dressed in a costume from the time of George Washington, only his white wig was dirty and falling over his ears. He seemed unaware of anything except what he was doing. And then she knew who it was. Yes, it was the profile she had seen on the chocolates sold everywhere in Salzburg –Mozart! Then, she looked more closely and saw the words "Violoncello Concerto" scribbled on top. "Oh, no! That's the lost manuscript," she thought. But at that moment, the vision disappeared.

CHAPTER THREE: THE MYSTERY UNFOLDS

"I have something really important to tell you," Kim whispered to Sam after they ate breakfast the next morning.

"Alright, what is it?" asked Sam when they were in Frau Huber's garden, out of Professor Stride's hearing range.

"Well, last night something really strange happened to me," continued Kim. "You know how I like to visualize things, like with that white dog?"

"Yeah, I never figured out how you could make him stop barking at us."

"This time," said Kim, "a strange vision came to me, without my even trying. I was just going to sleep when, all of a sudden, I saw myself dressed really weird, in old fashioned clothes, like from the time of Mozart."

"That's really cool," said Sam.

"What is even stranger is that I actually saw Mozart, and he was writing the cello concerto! It was right there before my very eyes!"

"Wow!" exclaimed Sam excitedly, "If you could see the manuscript then, maybe you can even see where the manuscript is now," said Sam.

"Do you think I should tell my father?"

"Why not? This could be important for him."

"But, what if he doesn't believe me?"

"Kimmy, you've got to try. He is your father, after all. You've got to trust him. You know, you need to have more confidence in yourself."

"I know, Sam. It's just that I've always felt so alone. I don't remember much about my mom, and I don't have any close relatives."

"I know. I've also been alone in my life, too. Just me and my mom. But, at least I have lots of cousins. That helps."

"You're lucky, Sam. I only have you as a friend."

"I'll always be here for you, Kimmy."

Kim felt reassured by Sam's words. He was like a brother to her – the brother she never had in real life.

From the garden, they walked out along the pebbled walkway, waiting for Professor Stride to return from town. He had finally received a phone call from Hauser and was hoping that the manuscript was found after all. Even a clue as to its whereabouts would be something to go on. When he got off the bus, however, he said that Hauser told him that in Vienna there was a list of two people who had been involved in its sale: the original owner and a smaller dealer. Hauser suspected that either one of them may have had second thoughts about selling it. Maybe they decided to have it stolen and returned to them. Or, perhaps some really wealthy buyer had heard of it and would only buy it directly from them. But, Hauser was unable to help Stride with the names or locations of the two.

Hauser had said, "The manuscript had been sent to me anonymously. The names of the two people selling it are being kept a secret at a lawyer's office in Vienna. As the potential buyer, only you have been given permission to know their identities." He then concluded, apologetically, "I'm afraid you'll have to go to Vienna personally."

Trying to make the best of a difficult situation, Professor Stride had told Hauser, "Well, at least it gives my daughter and her friend a chance to see other places in Austria."

After describing his conversation, Sam asked, "Does that mean we're going to Vienna?"

"Yes, it does," responded Stride anxiously, "Before we leave, however, I promised to talk with my friend, Karl Hess. I called him back after I talked to Hauser, and he told me to meet him at a café in the Mozartplatz this afternoon. First, we'll go back to the hotel to pack our bags."

While sitting on the bus going to town, Kim tried to broach the subject of her vision to her father.

"Dad, something very strange has been going on with me, and I'd like to tell you about it.

"What do you mean, Kim?"

Kim proceeded to describe her visions. She was almost in tears as she described the one of the child being thrown from a burning building. Then, she told him of the vision of Mozart she had the night before. To her surprise, instead of being skeptical, her father looked at her compassionately and said, "Don't worry, Kim, it will all become clearer in time."

Kim was amazed at her father's reaction. She had never seen him so open to her emotional outbursts before. Usually, he just closed himself off in his books and writings. Maybe being in Salzburg again was changing him.

Next, they went to the café to meet with Karl Hess. When he arrived, he looked concerned.

"I understand that Herr Hauser told you about the two people involved in selling the manuscript," Hess said. "I just want you to know I have some suspicions that he's not being entirely honest with you."

"You mean that he knows where the manuscript is after all?" asked Stride. He didn't want to start wandering all over Europe for no reason at all, much as he wanted Kim and Sam to enjoy themselves.

"Of that, I have no idea. I just wanted you to be very careful in talking to these people. You see, it was I who took it upon myself to notify you about the manuscript as soon as I looked at it after opening the mail. This was before Herr Hauser had seen it. When he found out that you were coming, he was quite displeased. He tried to hide it from me, but I could tell. I have reason to believe that he might arrange to have you followed. Now, don't worry about that. I've known him for many years. I very much doubt that he'd do anything to put you in danger, but he's obviously concerned about what you'll find out, so just be careful!"

"Thanks, Karl," said Stride, shaking his hand gratefully. He turned to Kim and Sam. "So, we're in for more than we expected, aren't we?" he smiled a little uneasily.

"You bet, Professor Stride!" said Sam.

"Oh Dad!" exclaimed Kim. "This is really going to be an adventure, isn't it?"

"I'm afraid so," said Stride, not looking forward to leaving his beloved Salzburg so soon after arriving. Then he said goodbye to his friend Karl and they were off. They took a bus that traveled along the Danube River towards Vienna. The river was sparkling in the sun, and small towns lay along its banks. Onion-shaped church steeples loomed above surrounding chalets whose balconies were overflowing with red geraniums.

When they reached Vienna, they stopped for a late lunch in an open-air restaurant in a park. All around them, tall stately buildings stood proudly, invoking the glories of the past. The atmosphere was one of regal elegance, so different from cozy Salzburg. "Dad, how did this cello concerto come to be written?" asked Kim.

"Well, in those days, usually a wealthy patron, such as a count or titled nobleman who played an instrument or had his own orchestra, would pay a known musician to write something for his instrument," said Stride.

"Who asked Mozart to write the cello concerto?" asked Sam.

"From what I have figured out, there was a Prince Karl Lichnowski who knew of Mozart from the court. He was probably the one who commissioned this work for a cellist he knew, but that, of course, is just speculation," said Stride. A cloud of hopelessness seemed to overwhelm him, and the children respectfully stopped asking him more questions.

"Now, I have to go to the law firm, just across from this park. Will you two meet me here in about an hour? They won't allow anyone but me inside to view the two names," said Stride.

"Sure, Dad," said Kim. "Don't worry about us. We may walk around a little, but we'll meet you back here in an hour." Stride got up, paid the bill and then left. Sam and Kim looked at each other, wondering where to go.

"Let's go for a walk around the park, Sam," Kim said. "Look at all the squirrels and birds we can feed with our leftover crumbs."

It was getting to be late afternoon, and a subdued feeling filled the park as activity was winding down. As they walked, the bells of a local church began to toll the hours. Kim, looking up at the tall buildings, was suddenly transfixed. Those clanging, mournful bells, the click-clop of a horse-drawn carriage on the cobble stone streets, the street lamps glimmering in the dusk— all of these sounds and sights transported her back to an earlier time in Vienna.

"Kimmy, what's happening to you?" cried Sam. "You seem so far away."

"What? Oh, don't worry. I just had one of those experiences again, like I was here before, a very long time ago."

"I was getting nervous about you. You seemed to be so out of it."

"I'm alright, Sam. It was very pleasant. I felt as if I were floating so high above everything, like I was being hugged by an older, timeless world."

"Well, I'm glad you're back on the ground again. Look, there's your dad coming out of that building. Let's go meet him."

Stride walked out of the building, looking very troubled. As he approached, he just motioned them to follow him. While walking, he said, "I must tell you that I am being followed. If you look over there, standing near the building I just exited, you'll see two men. I noticed them following me when I left the law office, and there they are again, trying to look inconspicuous!"

He nodded his head toward the two men standing next to the building. One was a very large man wearing a gray raincoat and the other was much smaller, with a pipe in his mouth.

"I don't think they're really dangerous. They probably have been hired by Herr Hauser to make sure I don't find out more than he wants me to. Just pretend you don't see them."

The two men glanced quickly in Stride's direction, and then looked away. Kim thought that they were funny, just like in a bad spy movie. She and Sam had

24

a hard time stifling a laugh. Then, to escape quickly, they jumped on an electric train stopping in front of them and traveled along the Ringstrasse to their hotel.

Sitting down to dinner that evening in a Hungarian restaurant specializing in goulash soup and thick farmer's bread, he told them about the two people on the list.

"One is a book and manuscript dealer from Venice," said Stride, "The other, the original owner, lives near Geneva, Switzerland. I hate to tell you this, but we may have to go to both these places to see these people in person. I feel like I'm dragging you two all over Europe. I'm so sorry."

"Oh, it doesn't feel like that at all! This is wonderful. We're getting to see all these awesome places," said Kim. "Everything here in Europe is so familiar, like I've been here before, and it's already a part of me."

"As for me, sir, I am really quite happy to go to all these great cities. It's a very exciting adventure." said Sam.

"Well, I'm glad you both see it that way,"

At this point, a violinist came among the tables playing gypsy music. The melody was spirited and exotic. They all momentarily forgot about the manuscript mystery and enjoyed the music, especially Stride, for whom music was his very life.

That evening, as Kim was going to sleep, visions again materialized before her closed eyes. *At first, she saw bright colors, like vivid turquoise and chartreuse pink. Then, she began to see figures, shadows at first, moving among the colors. She saw a woman playing the cello, her long skirts flowing over her knees to the ground. A divine melody rose from the cello, transporting Kim above the room so that she* could float and dance with it. *Never had she heard anything so enchanting. As she looked down at the music, she saw the same scribbling on the top of the page that she has seen in her previous vision.*

Suddenly, the sound of church bells interrupted the soaring melody. A child ran into the room, crying, "Mutti, shau," showing her cellist mother something in her hand. Although the mother spoke in German, strangely, Kim could still understand them.

"Was hast du da, mein Schatz?"

"I have a little frog, mother. I caught him at the pond. Isn't he beautiful?" asked the child.

"Yes, he is. And where will you keep him, my little Claudia?"

At that moment, a man, obviously the child's father came into the room dressed very elegantly. He took off his top hat and gloves, handing them to a maid scurrying behind him, who bowed and left the room.

"We had a pleasant time at the pond, didn't we Claudia?" he asked as he lovingly patted the child's head. "And, my dear Suzanna, have you been practicing the new cello concerto? Wasn't that a nice birthday gift that the Prince gave me for you? But, when would his musicians ever consent to play with a woman, even the Kapellmeister's own wife? There would be a mutiny on my hands if I compelled them. When will you ever have an orchestra to play it with?" he asked as he gave her a big hug.

"I don't mind, dear Helmut, I can imagine the orchestra parts. In any case, I don't think Herr Mozart will mind my playing it as a solo here at home," answered Suzanna.

"That may be, however, I would like to have a copy made of that score, just in case it may get soiled," said Helmut. "And I know the Prince will soon

expect a performance from my principal cellist," he added.

"Actually, my dear," replied Suzanna, "I'm sure my cousin Mathilda, who lives in Venice, would be so delighted to play the cello part also."

"Let me think about that, my darling," Helmut answered.

"She would love to hear Herr Mozart's music: just listen." Then she proceeded to play the first melody again on the cello.

The figures started receding and Kim felt that this lost manuscript must be found because the music she heard was so enchanting. If only she had her father's ability to hear any melody and be able to sing it back or write it down. With this thought, Kim drifted off to sleep.

CHAPTER FOUR: A VENETIAN MASQUERADE

The next morning, they were eating breakfast at their elegant Viennese hotel, with white tablecloths and real silver on the table. Kim found this to be the best time to tell Sam and her dad what she had experienced in her last vision.

"Dad, it was amazing," said Kim. "I saw this man, the music director, named Helmut, who said that the manuscript was given to him by the count as a birthday present for his wife, Suzanna. There was also a little girl named Claudia. It was such a sweet family. And, Suzanna wanted to send the concerto to her cousin Mathilde in Venice. But, it wasn't clear which she'd send: a copy or the original."

"Wow!" exclaimed Sam. "That's really cool. I wish I could have seen all that."

"Dad, what do you think about it?" asked Kim, expectantly.

"Well, it certainly fits. I mean, it could be true from what I've heard about the history of the manuscript," said Stride. "It seems that you may really have the ability to glimpse into past events." Then, he thought about it some more and added, "This might have been the person for whom the cello concerto was originally written, but how unusual for it to be a birthday present for the wife who was the cellist in the family."

"Why is it unusual, Dad?" asked Kim.

"In those days," he continued, "women were not taken seriously as artists or musicians. Even Mozart's talented sister, Nannerl, was overshadowed by her brilliant brother. Later, of course, Clara Schumann, a famous pianist, changed all that."

"It seems," said Sam, "as if Kim's visions are moving forward in time, Professor Stride. Her first vision was about Mozart writing the concerto, and now this one is about what happened to it after that. I can't wait to find out what happened to the manuscript next."

Kim looked a bit upset at this remark, saying, "Hey, guys, it's not like I can control what's happening to me. It just pops up on its own."

"There's no pressure on you, Kim," said Stride. "In any case, we must travel again. Which will it be first – Venice or Geneva?"

"Venice, of course," Sam suggested, "with gondolas floating on canals and Italian ices and..."

"Yes, that's what I was thinking also," said Kim.

"So, Venice it is," said Stride.

While taking the train down to Venice, they started noticing the differences between Austria and Italy. In Austria, the houses were well kept, and the gardens were neatly tended. As soon as they crossed the border into Italy, the houses looked like they were slowly crumbling with the passage of time. Weeds and flowers grew up along the cracks in roadways and door thresholds. It was as if people's attitudes changed from taking control over nature to letting it completely go its own way.

The travelers enjoyed the lilt of the Italian language as they heard new passengers getting on.

An old woman with twinkling eyes came to sit on one of the empty seats in their compartment. She looked a little disheveled, and as soon as she sat down, she took out some thick Italian bread and cheese, offering some of it to them before she ate. "*Mangia*, eat," she said. They passed it around, breaking off chunks and hungrily biting into the crusty bread and strong-smelling cheese.

When the train arrived in Venice, they couldn't wait to get on a boat, but first they checked into a hotel near the station and stored their bags.

"Let's take a vaporetto," said Stride. "A gondola is so expensive, and this will get us to St. Mark's Square just as easily." So, they jumped across the water gap onto the bus-like boat meant for workers and cost-conscious tourists.

The canal looked a little murky as the vaporetto gently plowed its way through the water, making small rivulets behind it. Then, the full fantasy of that day loomed up before them as they saw the gray forms of the buildings rising up from the water like ghosts. Graceful black gondolas were everywhere, some tied to gaily red-and-white-striped poles emerging from the water near the buildings. As they neared the St. Mark's Square boat landing, they could begin to make out the ironwork filigree of the balconies. Everything was undulating and sparkling from the surrounding water.

St. Mark's Square was imposing in a different way than the sights in Vienna. Here, the ornate buildings spoke of a merry, voluptuous past. The days of Venice's sensuous trading in silks, spices and other Eastern goods permeated the air. The ornate cream-colored buildings and the huge square where sumptuous operas were held recalled days of rich luxury. The three adventurers rambled into the side streets where small restaurants and shops hugged each other in crumbling friendship. Stopping for a gelato, the creamy Italian ice cream, they sat on tall stools and looked at the festive masks sold in the shop opposite them.

"They must have a lot of parties around here, especially masked balls, I bet," said Sam.

"Yes, this city seems to thrive on celebration and mystery," said Stride. "Speaking of mysteries, the book dealer lives right on the next street. We'd better find out what he knows, but remember, I have to play dumb so he isn't suspicious. He might tip me off to the whereabouts of the manuscript. Remember Karl Hess' warning. This man will probably pretend that he doesn't know anything at all."

"Don't worry, Professor Stride. Kim and I are getting good at pretending things. We'll have our very own masked party, only without masks," said Sam. So, they went off to find the small shop specializing in old music manuscripts. As they entered the shop, a little bell tinkled at the top of the door, and a parrot in a cage screamed out, "*Guarda, guarda, pericoloso.*"

"What does that mean?" asked Sam.

"He just said, 'watch out, it's dangerous,'" said Stride.

"Buon giorno, may I help you?" asked an elderly man behind the counter.

"How does he know that we're American?" whispered Kim to her dad.

"Our clothes," he replied.

"Yes, I would like to buy something very old, an original music manuscript. Have you got anything I could look at?" Stride asked the man.

"Yes, of course," answered the man in a thick Italian accent. "My name is Romano, the owner of this shop. I am happy to help you. Do you have anything special in mind?"

"Well, I would like something written for cello," answered Stride.

"We have some very old cello sonatas written in the 19th century," Romano said.

"I was hoping for something older, maybe in the 18th century and preferably a concerto," continued Stride.

"Well, you know, Signore, that there were only a very few written that early," he said.

"Oh. What would they be?" queried Stride.

"Haydn wrote a few, and there's a rumor that even Mozart may have written one, but, unfortunately that has been lost," said Romano, cagily.

"Is there no hope of finding it?" asked Stride.

"Signore, if it still existed, it would cost millions. Would you be prepared to pay that much for it?" asked Romano.

"Yes, of course. If it were available, that is."

"Let me give you a card, Signore, for a colleague of mine who can help you. I believe she might have the very thing you are looking for." Romano disappeared behind the counter and returned with a well-worn card, which he handed to Stride.

"Thank you very much, Signor Romano. I am much indebted to you," replied Stride. Then, he signaled Kim and Sam, silently leading them out of the shop. After walking to the next block and sitting by the edge of a canal, they both started to question Stride at once.

"Why didn't you tell him who you really were?" asked Sam.

"Because I wanted to see if he had the manuscript to sell. If he had it, he would want to sell it secretly, so that he would not be discovered," answered Stride.

"Do you think he really has the manuscript, then?" asked Kim.

"I don't know. If he did, he might have hinted at it. But this card might tell us more. Stride took out the card and started to read it to them, but then stopped.

"What does it say, Dad?" asked Kim.

"It says, 'Otto and Mathilde Groschen, Dealers in Fine Manuscripts, 11 Rue de Marchande, Nyon, Switzerland.' Of course, that's the other name I got from the lawyer's office. She's supposed to have been the original owner!"

"That name, Mathilde, sounds familiar," said Kim.

"Isn't that the cousin's name, from your dream, Kim?" said Sam. "But she would be way too old to still be living today,"

"Well, you know," mused Stride, "in old families, a name is passed down from child to child through a long line of ancestors. She could be related to the original cousin in Venice who received the Mozart manuscript."

"Does that mean we are taking the next train to Geneva?" asked Sam, who was ready for the next adventure.

"You bet, since we are headed there anyway. I guess this man is not the one we are looking for, unless...," mused Stride.

"Unless what?" asked Sam.

"Unless he is leading us on a wild goose chase, or he knows the owner has stolen it back," replied Stride. "In any case, we aren't going to get any more out of him, so let's go on."

"Shouldn't we phone ahead?" suggested Sam.

"If Mrs. Groschen is involved in stealing back the manuscript, my phone call would tip her off," explained Stride.

"But if Romano is also in on it, wouldn't he call

ahead?" asked Kim.

"Well, we might be able to sense that when we meet her, but we have to follow this lead," said Stride, convinced he was going in the right direction. Again, they packed their bags and took the next train for Geneva, by way of Milano. Then, they'd have to change trains in Geneva on the way to Nyon. Since they took a night coach for such a long ride, Kim slept in the upper bunk of a very noisy, small bed.

Before drifting off to sleep, however, she had another vision: *flames were engulfing a beautiful room! She heard cries as people ran out of the burning building, and she saw high up the figure of a man stuffing a manuscript into a child's jacket and then tossing her out a window! Then she heard the man cry out, "Thanks be to God, they've caught her!"*

Flames rose up before Kim's eyes.

Terrified, she woke up, but all was dark, and the train kept rattling along toward Geneva.

CHAPTER FIVE: THE MANUSCRIPT REAPPEARS

The next morning, they boarded the train for Nyon, which chugged along, hugging the sparkling Lake of Geneva. On the other side of the lake, they could see the snow-capped Alps in the distance.

"Dad, do you think we can visit the Alps while we're here? I used to love reading Heidi when I was young," asked Kim. "Do you remember?"

"I don't see why we can't stop for a quick visit," Stride replied.

"I would also love to see the Jungfrau," added Sam. "I read that it's one of the highest snow-capped mountains in Switzerland."

"It looks like that's what we'll do next, as soon as we check out this address," replied Stride. "Let's stop here."

They jumped off and wandered among the side streets with the card, locating an apartment building. As they rang the bell, a sweet-looking elderly woman stood at the top of the stairs. "Entrez," she said. She welcomed them into her apartment and explained to them that her friend, Romano, had phoned her and told her that they might be coming soon.

So, if she's got the manuscript, she's going to be very devious, thought Stride.

"You are very welcome here," she said in distinct, if heavily-accented English. "I understand that you are interested in buying a manuscript of a Mozart cello concerto."

"Well, actually," he replied, "I would like to look at it first to check its authenticity. Do you know where it is?"

Stride was a little surprised that she would so easily admit that Romano had been in contact with her, but he knew he had to play along.

"I've been told by Signore Romano that it's being offered for sale for me by a Herr Hauser in Salzburg. It was forwarded by special courier a while ago. I have heard nothing more about it since. Didn't Signore Romano tell you?" she asked innocently.

"I guess I didn't make my intentions clear," said Stride. "No matter. I'm sure you'll provide me with Herr Hauser's address. In any case, before I go any further in possibly buying it, I wanted to meet you in person to learn more about it. After all, you would best know its history."

Obviously, either she or Romano was lying. Or, perhaps it was both of them? In any case, Stride thought he'd better not disclose that Hauser had reported the manuscript missing. Perhaps Frau Groschen might reveal something.

"What about it would you like to know, Monsieur?" she hesitated.

Oh, excuse me for my lack of manners," said Stride. He had been so preoccupied that he'd forgotten to introduce himself, Kim and Sam.

"I am Daniel Stride, and this is my daughter, Kim, and her friend, Sam."

"Such charming young people," said their hostess. "And now, how may I enlighten you about the concerto?"

"Could you tell me something of its origins?" Stride asked her.

"Actually, a cellist cousin in Vienna, named Suzanna, originally had the manuscript and sent it to a great aunt four generations ago where she lived in Venice."

"Was the great aunt also named Mathilde?" asked Kim.

"Yes, she was. And she also played cello. So Mathilde must have been very happy to receive that music. But, we were never sure if it was the original or a copy," added Frau Groschen.

"Were you never able to find out?" asked Stride.

"There was a fire in the house, and the cousin and her family all died. That is, except for one of the children. But, my family lost all contact with her. It was rumored that she had the other manuscript."

"Do you mean that Suzanna and Helmut, except for little Claudia, all died?" asked Kim, unable to hide her concern.

"Yes, it was quite a tragedy. They think it was a cinder from the fireplace that started the fire," said Frau Groschen, "How did you know all their names?"

"My daughter is interested in genealogy and has learned quite a bit that way," said Stride quickly.

"But, don't you know that manuscript was . . .?" Sam began to blurt out, forgetting himself.

"... quite valuable?" interrupted Stride, giving Sam a warning look which silenced him.

"Yes. In fact, we never understood its value until a cousin of mine was looking over it several months ago. At that time, we realized that it was the manuscript that we had heard about as children, but we had never known its exact whereabouts. We didn't know that this was the missing Mozart cello concerto. You see, there is no signature anywhere. It can only be determined as authentic at this point by the distinctive style. And once we understood what it was, my husband and I wanted the world to see it as soon as possible. It was then that I notified Signore Romano," she explained.

"Thank you so much, Frau Groschen. It was certainly worthwhile hearing the story in your own words," said Stride.

"Now, we are going to travel to the Alps and then back to Salzburg, where I will discuss the possible purchase of the manuscript with Herr Hauser," said Stride.

Before they left, Stride, Kim and Sam spent a while longer with Frau Groschen, who kindly gave them some advice on the best way to visit the Alps. Stride was hoping that the old woman might make some slip that would give him a clue as to where to look next. But, either Frau Groschen knew nothing or she was quite the actress. In order to play along with the act, Stride asked her for Hauser's address before they left.

As they left the apartment building, Kim asked, "Did you pick up anything from her that might help us find out where it is?"

Stride looked puzzled and shrugged.

"I have a feeling that Karl's right. Hauser wasn't very pleased to see me in the first place. But, I also sense that Hauser knew these two people and is buying time by sending me to find them. The question is why? Unless . . . maybe he had another buyer. Don't worry; we'll get to the bottom of this. Even if we do find the manuscript, it may be only a copy! It would still be valuable, of course, but not nearly as precious as one in Mozart's own handwriting!"

"Do you think she was at least telling the truth about the fire?" Sam asked.

"Oh, yes," said Kim. "I saw it!"

"You what?" asked Sam and Stride together.

"I actually saw the child, little Claudia, being thrown from the window with the manuscript! Dad, I just realized, that was my first vision! Now, I understand what I saw that very first time, before we even left for Salzburg. I saw a terrified child falling through fiery air with old parchment paper stuffed in her jacket!"

"You saw this even before we left for Salzburg? Even before we knew anything about the manuscript being missing?" asked Sam. "Why didn't you tell me anything about it?"

"Because I was just so confused. It didn't make any sense or relate to anything I recognized," added Kim. "Now, it all fits together."

"It seems that you had a premonition of what was going to happen from the beginning," said Stride.

"Yes, now I can see that. At the time, I was just terrified," said Kim.

"Well, now that you've sorted that out, I wonder what's next?" said Sam.

"The Alps! That's what's next," cried Kim joyfully.

They took the next boat ride on Lake Geneva, passing the Castle of Chillon on the way to Lausanne, where they took a train to Interlaken at the foot of the Alps. As they rode along, they saw the endless grape vineyards running upwards from the water's edge and the gleaming lake recede in the background as the train climbed up the hills into the green mountains. While looking out the window, however, Kim had the feeling that two men in one of the cars driving alongside the road looked like the ones who were following them in Vienna.

Once in Interlaken, they took a mountain train to Lauterbrunnen, where they stayed in a youth hostel

Lauterbrunnen

near the station. These youth hostels were basically dormitories for traveling young people, but this one also had separate rooms for families.

Lauterbrunnen was surrounded by high mountains cradling the valley, with a very high waterfall known as the Staubbach Falls (or "Horse's Tail") cascading from the top of one of the bluffs. Kim felt like she was in a fantasy world as she gazed at the ring of mountains around her. Since it was already evening when they arrived, they just ate some bread and cheese for supper. While eating, they were discussing the meaning of Kim's previous visions when Sam asked, "Do you think we really might be looking for two manuscripts?"

"That seems very unlikely," said Stride. "Still, Kim, do you think your vision of the falling child might have given us a sign that the original manuscript still exists? The one that was in Groschen's possession may have been a copy sent to the cousin in Venice. Of course, we wouldn't know which one is the original unless I had a chance to examine at least one of them. Mozart had a very distinct notation that couldn't possibly be copied. You might have given us a lead to that original one." Kim agreed, but she really hadn't much to say.

That night, she was overwhelmed with sadness as she again recalled Frau Groschen's words about that lovely family, especially Suzanna and little Claudia with her frog. Her only consolation was that the little girl survived. Then, sometime during the night, a vision came to her that she didn't understand at all.

After swirling lights of pink and lavender receded, figures emerged inside a room with bare wooden walls. An older woman in a long black dress was playing a piano piece that Kim had heard before — Schumann's "Arabesque." While she was playing, a younger woman entered the room. Her dark hair was pulled back, and she, too, wore a long dark dress and a serious look on her face. The older woman stopped playing, turned, and smiled as the young woman spoke.

"Mother, you just received an envelope from the daughter of a woman who was once your student. It contains a manuscript and a letter, which says that

she appreciated your instruction of her so much that her mother left you this manuscript in her will. It is thought to be written by a contemporary of Mozart's," *she said.*

"What was this pupil's name, my dear Marie?" asked the woman at the piano.

"Let me see," said Marie as she examined the signature. "The name is Claudia Müller.

"Oh, yes, I remember teaching a Claudia Waldheim Müller. She was the granddaughter of a Kapellmeister during Mozart's time. She told me that her mother was brought up by an aunt after her parents tragically died in a fire. Leave it on the table, dear, and I will look it over," said the woman in black. "Perhaps Brahms would like to see it as well," she added.

Then the vision grew dark and faded into the morning light.

CHAPTER SIX: ALPINE PURSUIT

They got up early the next morning in order to visit Mürren, a little town perched high on the mountain facing the Jungfrau. At breakfast, Kim told them about her last vision of a woman in black at the piano who received the manuscript. Stride was quite excited.

"The woman you saw, Kim," said Stride, "seems to be none other than Clara Schumann, the great pianist. The 'Brahms' she referred to was Johannes Brahms, the eminent German composer. I just wonder why he didn't find out the manuscript's true value?"

"Maybe they just forgot to show him," suggested Sam.

"Well, it's possible that Kim's visions will tell us more," said Stride, giving Kim a confident smile.

Kim just shrugged. She knew she couldn't get her visions to come to her whenever she wanted, but she did want to please her father. And, what if her visions led him off track? Then, he wouldn't be so pleased with her. She just didn't want to let him down.

After packing their knapsacks with drinks and granola bars, they took the funicular railway up to the Grütschalp station.

"Look, Dad, how this train climbs along the steep

mountain. I hope the cable doesn't break," said Kim nervously.

"Don't worry, Kim, the Swiss are famous for the way they take care of all their cables. You noticed how all the trains were exactly on time whenever we made connections? That's part of Swiss precision," said Stride.

In the compartment in front of them, they suddenly caught sight of the undercover men they had seen following them in Vienna. Their hats were slanted over their faces to hide their identities.

"It looks like those two are following us again," remarked Sam. "I wonder if we'll be able to go anywhere without them."

"Well, maybe we can lose them somewhere along the way," said Stride.

From there, they took another short train ride along the ridge, facing the majestic, sparkling-white trio of mountains — the Jungfrau, the Eiger and the Mönch. Once arriving in Mürren, they started walking through the little town. Suddenly, they heard a deep, sad sound, but they couldn't tell where it was coming from.

"Professor Stride, what is that sound?" asked Sam.

"Those are Alpine horns, two of them in fact, harmonizing," said Stride.

"They sound haunting to me," said Kim. "And, they're echoing around the valley as we walk."

"Yes, they are those very long horns, about twelve feet or so. They make a very deep sound that bounces off the mountains."

They hiked the mountain path to Gimmelwald, reachable only on foot, with the blazing, snow-covered Alps in front of them. All around them, they saw sloping meadows dotted with chalet farms and grazing goats.

The two men who had been following them all this

Gimmelwald

time were now far behind, puffing hard and visibly tired. Stride shared a little laugh at the not-very-subtle "undercover" men, saying, "I'll bet we'll lose them before we get to Gimmelwald."

"I hear bells ringing, but I can't figure out where they're coming from," said Kim.

"Those are cowbells, Kim," answered Stride. "Did you notice that there is a head cow with a deep-clanging bell? The smaller bells belong to the other cows in the herd. In that way, the herd knows the different sound of their leader and can follow her."

When they reached Gimmelwald, they found an outdoor restaurant and sat in the warm sun under colorful umbrellas. They heard multiple languages spoken by fellow hikers, mostly Swiss-French and

Swiss-German.

"How come there seem to be only Swiss people up here, Dad?" asked Kim.

"I think that most other tourists prefer not to exert themselves to get to places like this," said Stride. "Or else not too many foreigners know about this place. All right, let's eat. What kind of dishes do they have?"

They ordered spaghetti and sauce, since it was the cheapest dish on the menu. Stride realized that with all of their extra traveling, they had to tighten their budget.

While they were waiting for their meals, Kim asked her dad about Clara Schumann. "Could you tell us more about this old lady in my dream?" she asked.

"Sure, Kim," he answered. "Clara Schumann was married to a very famous composer, Robert Schumann. She loved her late husband's music and played it frequently at her concerts throughout Germany, France, Switzerland, England and even Russia. Many of Clara's admirers sent her presents of jewelry or even manuscripts in appreciation of her wonderful musical interpretations. I find it amazing that your mind can recreate the past like this, without even knowing who you're seeing. And the facts are always accurate, like her eldest daughter's name — Marie," he added.

"And, Kim seems to be following the manuscript's journey too," added Sam.

"Yes, you're right Sam," said Stride.

"But Dad, I still don't know where this lady Clara Schumann was or what happened to the manuscript after she got it," added Kim, as steaming bowls of spaghetti and sauce arrived.

They feasted, and then took the lift down to the valley of Lauterbrunnen followed by a bus ride to the youth hostel. On the way, they passed the underground cavern where swirling water rushed through, creating a loud roar.

"Now you know where Lauterbrunnen gets its name," said Stride. "'Laut' means noisy or ringing and 'brunnen' means 'fountain' or 'well'. Hence, 'noisy fountain.'"

Once back at the youth hostel, happily exhausted from having fulfilled a childhood wish to visit the Alps, Kim went to bed, dreaming of snow-capped mountains, grazing goats and deep green valleys. She kept thinking, however, about her perplexing vision of the night before. What happened to the manuscript after it had been given to Clara Schumann? And where were the Schumanns living when the manuscript was sent to her? Who sent it? Was it really the granddaughter of the same Claudia who had survived the fire? Was the manuscript the missing cello concerto? As she thought of these questions, she drifted off to sleep.

Suddenly, in the middle of the night, the colors preceding her visions came back — this time an aqua blue swirling around figures. *She was seeing the back of a woman's head looking out the window. What she saw was a sparkling lake and snow-capped mountains beyond it, seeming to rise out of the water. The woman turned around and spoke to someone in the room.*

"Shall we take mother out for a walk in the countryside today, Elise?"

"But how can we, Marie? You know she cannot manage long distances anymore," answered Elise.

"We can use the wheelchair. You know how much she loves to be outdoors," continued Maria.

"Alright, if you think she will not be too tired by the journey," agreed Elise. "I'm glad she's finally getting around to looking at that manuscript. It might be really

valuable," she said, pointing to an old parchment wrapped in cloth which lay on the table.

"Well," said Marie with a sigh, "she's spent so much time editing Poppa's music that she has never much bothered with anyone else's work."

Then Kim saw them taking their mother, whom she now recognized as Clara Schumann, in a wheelchair onto a path along the lake. After they left, a younger woman dressed in a maid's outfit tiptoed into the room looking around very cautiously. Seeing the manuscript on the table, the young woman snatched it and placed it under her apron. Then she ran out of the room.

Kim awoke startled. So, that's what happened to the manuscript! The house was somewhere beside a lake and in front of high mountains. Why, they must be the Alps! I have to tell father in the morning.

CHAPTER SEVEN: A VERY NARROW ESCAPE

"We seem to have reached a dead end in our search for the manuscript," said Stride. "I don't really know where to go next. Maybe we should just return to Salzburg and enjoy the rest of the month there."

As the morning sun rose over the snow-capped mountains encircling the valley, Kim, Sam and Stride were having breakfast out on the balcony so that they could enjoy the sparkling Alps.

"But, I had another vision last night, and I know what happened to the manuscript," said Kim.

"Another vision? Cool! What did you see?" asked Sam.

"Well, I saw the Schumanns again, and when Clara and her daughters went on a walk, a maid servant stole the manuscript. She hid the manuscript under her apron and sneaked out of the room. I also saw a calendar on the wall. It showed July 18, 1895. They were living in a town off a lake with this same Alpine range in the distance," said Kim.

"I know of such a town where Clara Schumann and her daughters probably stayed. It's called Brienz which is on the Brienzersee, a lake to the east of Interlaken."

"Can we go there now, Dad?" asked Kim.

"Sure, we can," answered Stride. "It's actually on our way back towards Salzburg. Why don't we stop and see where your visions take us from there?"

Kim was delighted that her father seemed to trust her visions and now even depended on them for the next step of their journey. She also was amazed that he seemed to know so much about music history and Europe.

"Dad, I'm really happy that you understand me and accept these visions so totally now. It means a lot to me to have something that I can do for you."

"Actually, you remind me a lot of your mother in this way. Did you know that she had this talent as well?"

"I didn't know that, Dad. What kind of visions did she have?"

"Well, like you, she was able to see things in the past and before they happened in the future. She even foresaw her own...." At this point Stride closed his eyes and held back tears.

Sam and Kim didn't say anything. They wanted to respect his private feelings. After a few quiet moments, they went back to the youth hostel, packed their bags, and headed for the train to Interlaken. There, they changed to a local train to Brienz, only about twenty minutes farther along the lake.

Kim recognized the lake as being the one she saw in her vision. The Alps gleamed in the background, and the water sparkled as boats of all kinds, including sailboats, small cruise boats and rowboats, floated in the sun. The small villages dotting the shoreline looked like sleepy hamlets in fairy tales she had read as a child. She never dreamed that they could be real, and that's why everything she was experiencing felt like a dream.

When they reached Brienz, they noticed odd

woodcarvings everywhere — on the boat landing and in the small shops along the main road hugging the shoreline.

"Professor Stride, this town seems to be different from the others we've seen, more like living in a folktale," said Sam, taking in all the details of the lakeside town.

"You're right, Sam," Stride answered. "This town is famous for its woodcarvings. The artists live in this town and neighboring ones around the lake. They especially like to make carvings of animals and even created a wild animal preserve on top of the hill in the woods. That way, they could study the native deer and other animals in order to carve them accurately."

"Have you ever been there?" asked Sam, curious.

"Yes, I have, Sam. To tell you the truth, I found it a little sad for wild animals to be kept in captivity like that," added Stride.

They decided to eat at an outdoor restaurant right by the water's edge so that they could have a full view of the lake and mountains. They ordered big salads, some with tuna fish in the center of the dish, called "fitness salads." As a side dish, they had the hearty whole grain bread found everywhere in the country. When she was done eating and watching the water lapping against the wood platform of the restaurant, Kim drifted into her "knowing" space, as she was beginning to recognize it. Soothed by the water, the sunshine and the distant mountains, she momentarily closed her eyes and saw a figure. *It was the young maid who had taken the manuscript. She somehow sensed that it was here, in this town, that the Schumann family had stayed and where the maid had lived. Then, she saw the woman with a man, giving him the cherished manuscript.*

"Here, Johannes, give it to Father to sell to one of

his clients. Then, we can have some decent meals."
"How can I do that? If he knows it was taken, he would send me away. I would dishonor the Jürgen name," he replied.
"Just tell him that someone gave it to you. That would be the truth," she replied. Then the vision faded. Slowly, Kim drifted back to the present and opened her eyes to find both Sam and her father watching her intently.

"Kim, what have you seen?" asked Sam.

"How did you know?" answered Kim.

"Oh, we can now clearly tell when you are mind-traveling, Kim," said her father.

"You can? Sometimes I don't even know myself," answered Kim. "Dad, do you think that we can stay here for tonight?" asked Kim. "The name Jürgen was mentioned in my last vision. It's the family name of the woman who stole the manuscript. I think that they lived in this town."

"Why not? This is a very pleasant spot. We can ask for the name of a bed and breakfast at the tourist center across from the train station," he answered.

The tourist center sent them to a chalet at the edge of town. The landlady was a friendly woman with white hair, who showed them into rooms all sharing a balcony facing the lake and mountains.

"No wonder Clara Schumann and her daughters liked to spend their summers in this region. In fact, after Clara died, her daughter Marie moved to nearby Interlaken to live permanently," said Stride.

That evening, the landlady, Frau Grüber, invited them to a wine and cheese party. Kim and Sam drank herbal tea with their bread and cheese, while Stride enjoyed the local wine. The other guests were also there speaking in Swiss-German, which Stride could barely understand, although he spoke fluent German.

Before going to bed, however, he spoke to the landlady.

"Thank you, Frau Grüber, for inviting us to your party. By the way, do you happen to know anyone in town by the name of Jürgen?

"Oh, ya. They live in a big chalet in town, near da' church with carvings of disciples on da' tower," she answered in her broken English.

"Thank you again," he said.

The next morning, Frau Grüber presented Kim and Sam with two soft-boiled eggs after finding out that they liked eggs for breakfast.

"Ya, you like? From chickens in yard, d'ey lay d'is morning. Very fresh," she said presenting them to Kim and Sam.

"These are the best eggs I have ever eaten," said Sam.

"Happy chickens," replied Kim. "They must like the lake view."

After breakfast, they went hiking through the town again, this time searching for the church with the carved disciples. Finally, in back of the main road, high upon the sloping mountain, they found it. There was a woodshop attached to the big chalet near the church that the landlady described. It was surrounded by a garden growing all around the walls. Red hollyhocks stood tall against the sides of the windows, looking very much like the fairy tale cottages from Kim's childhood books.

As they entered, a little bell jingled, and they were invited inside by an old man with twinkling eyes. There were wood shavings strewn on the floor and wooden sculptures, as well as carvings of animals on the tables.

While Stride was asking questions of the shopkeeper, as if to buy a wooden sculpture, Kim and

Sam wandered among the various cuttings, carvings of animals, whimsical signs for shopkeepers

Brienz Woodshop

and frames cut out to reveal the interiors of farmhouses, mostly kitchens.

On one of the shelves along the wall, Kim saw something that caught her eye. It was a carving of a young woman playing the cello. It was so delicately done, every feature of the face and loving embrace of the cello expressed the artist's vision. She picked it up and was hypnotized by it. As she held it, she felt a strange tingling in her fingers and felt transported to another time and place. This piece was calling to her with some secret message. But, she needed privacy and this was not the place for the revelations within it. At once, she brought it to her father.

"This is the piece we must buy, Dad. Look how beautifully carved it is," she said. Stride looked it over, saying, "Yes, I see what you mean, Kim." Then facing the shopkeeper, he asked, "We would like to buy this sculpture. Would you please tell me how much it costs?"

"I will have to ask the owner," he replied, and, excusing himself, went behind to a back room. They could hear a murmur of voices. Then from behind the door came the shopkeeper and an ancient-looking man, though still very lively and strong.

"Hello. I am Christian Jürgen. I understand that you are interested in buying something in my shop," he said, shaking hands with Stride.

"Well yes, Herr Jürgen. Actually I am interested in the carving of the cello player," replied Stride.

"I am sorry to tell you that this piece is not for sale. It is a mistake that it was in the shop. Can I interest you in something else?" asked Herr Jürgen.

"Not exactly. You see, my daughter has taken a particular liking to this one piece, and I would really like to buy it for her," continued Stride.

"You must understand that this carving has been in my family for a long time. It has a special sentimental value. I am sorry to disappoint you," continued Jurgen. "However, I would be happy to give you a discount on anything else you see here. Perhaps this lovely Steinbock? It is very beautiful, don't you think, young lady?" he asked Kim, holding the carving of a mountain deer up to her.

"Er, no thank you, Herr Jürgen," replied Kim.

"Well, then, I am sorry. It is out of the question for me to sell the other piece," he replied firmly, leading them to the door. "Perhaps you would like to come back at another time," he added.

When the door shut behind them, the travelers

gathered at the street corner, considering their options. "I don't think this is going to work. I'm really sorry, Kim," said Stride. "You know that I was ready to buy it for you."

"That's all right, Dad. I know," Kim answered. "Forget it."

After leaving the shop, they started walking down the hill towards the lake. While Stride stopped by the side of the road to take some photos of the church, Sam and Kim were waiting for him farther down the roadway. Feeling frustrated, Sam asked, "How can you just forget it, Kim? You know the effect it had on you. It was ready to give you a vision. I could just tell from the look on your face. You must have that cellist sculpture!"

"Calm down, Sam," replied Kim. "You could see how Herr Jürgen was not about to give in. It seemed as if there was something he wanted to hide about it."

"Maybe if you can't buy it, you can borrow it for a while?"

"I don't think that he would even let us borrow it, Sam."

"Well, I guess you're right. I just feel so disappointed," said Sam.

"I do, too, Sam," added Kim.

That afternoon, they went on a special cruise around the lake, enjoying the summer breezes as the boat glided along, leaving a soothing wake behind it. Everything was perfect. The water looked like stars dancing on its surface, the snow glistening on the Alps, and the quaint villages where the cruise stopped to take on more passengers. While Stride was taking pictures at one end of the boat, Kim and Sam found that they could resume their talk.

"I really think that you should at least give another shot at that cellist carving," said Sam. "Maybe it would reveal something really important to you."

"I know, Sam, I felt that too," answered Kim. "But how?"

"I have an idea," said Sam. "Maybe we could go into the shop while everyone is sleeping and you could just hold it for a while. I could keep watch and…"

"Wait a minute, Sam," said Kim, "Don't you think that they would be putting it somewhere else after that? Maybe somewhere secret, and then we would never find it?"

"Well, do you have any better ideas?" he asked.

"No, not really," said Kim.

"It's worth a try," he answered.

"My dad would never allow that anyway. He is Mr. Do Right, if you know what I mean. He would never forgive me if he found out or if we got into trouble with the police for illegal entry," said Kim. She dreaded to think of the consequences if her dad were called by the police in the middle of the night about his delinquent daughter.

"Maybe you're right, but it's so important for him to find this manuscript. You would be doing him a favor," said Sam.

Stride was returning to their side of the boat, so Kim and Sam looked out over the water as if they hadn't a care in the world. "To be continued," whispered Sam.

"I hope you two are not too bored. I'm afraid there's not much to do on a boat ride except just sit and look at the landscape," said Stride.

"It's alright, Dad. Actually, it's a soothing thing to do after being practically thrown out of a shop just for wanting to buy something," said Kim.

"Yes, that's unfortunate," said Stride. "Let's just forget it and think about what we'll do next or where we'll go tomorrow morning," said Stride. "Maybe you'll have another vision that will tell us where the manuscript is after all. Though I could tell that the sculpture was important to you, so far you haven't needed any physical object to give you these glimpses."

"You're right, Dad," said Kim. "I need to just rely on myself."

After returning from the boat trip and deciding to leave in the morning for Luzern, they went to bed early. During the night, however, Kim saw a strange form enter her balcony. She was about to scream when she heard "Shhh. It's me, Sam."

"What are you doing here, Sam?" she asked.

"Listen Kim, the more I think about it, the more I am sure that you should enter the shop and hold the sculpture," he said.

"What makes you think we could get away with it?" asked Kim.

"I just feel that if you don't take this opportunity to try, you'll regret it for the rest of your life," he said.

"I know you're right, but I have never done something like this before," said Kim. "I mean, going behind my dad's back like this."

"But, you are doing it for him," said Sam. "He needs to find that manuscript. Otherwise, he's going to have a hard time justifying spending all this University money."

"Okay, I'll do it for my father," said Kim. "You know I'd do anything for him."

"Yes, I know. He's been really good to me, too." said Sam.

In the middle of the night, the two adventurers quietly sneaked out of the room, carefully leaving the entry door open so that they could get back in without a key. Then, they walked along the main street to the wood shop.

The gigantic Alps across the lake were gleaming in the moonlight. Lake water was lapping against boats moored for the night. No one was out. The only sounds were the owls in the trees and the crickets in the backyard gardens.

"Sam, are there any wolves around here?" asked Kim, shaking with fear.

"If there are, I don't think they would come into the town, Kim," he answered reassuringly.

Finally, they walked up the hill to the wood shop. Stealthily, they looked into the shop windows, noticing that one had been left ajar, probably to let in the family cat.

"Alright Kim, do you want to go through the window and I'll stay outside to warn you if anyone approaches?" asked Sam.

"I guess so," answered Kim, scared, but also feeling ready to begin.

She slowly opened the window a little more, and Sam hoisted her up by making a footing for her with his hands. Since she was so thin, she readily slipped through the window and into the shop. All was quiet as she jumped down onto the floor and walked to the spot where she first saw the sculpture of the cellist. And there it still was! She couldn't believe her good luck! She slowly lifted it off the shelf with both her hands. Again, she felt that tingling sensation from touching it. Then, a scene appeared before her.

Kim saw two figures, one was an old man and the other was younger, possibly Johannes, whom she had seen in the previous vision. The old man was bitter and angrily shouting, "You have put a curse on this family! See how your sister has been left paralyzed by your actions? You have concealed this crime from me for almost twenty years and now see how God has punished her. Why did you take it?"

Johannes stammered, frightened by his father's anger. "She did it to help the family when we were in such need, but as soon as she did so, we realized that if the theft had been reported by such a prominent family as the Schumanns, any collector interested in buying it would know about it and report us. I only revealed this to you now because the disappearance of the manuscript must have been forgotten after all this time, and we need the money to treat Katrina's illness."

"Well, it's taken twenty years, but now that she's fully paralyzed, you can see God's curse has been delivered upon her head," thundered the old man.

"But, Father, that is a coincidence, not a curse," answered Johannes.

"However you see it," said the old man, "you are banished from my house and this town. Just leave, now."

"Not without taking Katrina with me," replied Johannes. "I know of a chapel in Seelisberg where many of the afflicted who were paralyzed have been healed. I will bring her there to be cured."

"The two of you are in this together. Just go. I never want to see you again," his father said furiously. An old woman was crying in the shadows of the room. Suddenly, the whole room blazed with an ethereal light. Kim almost dropped the sculpture, but managed to place it back on the shelf.

"Hurry, I see a light on upstairs," Sam whispered loudly from the window.

It was too late. Kim had to hide quickly. Someone was coming down the stairs. She saw a table with a bench and crawled underneath it. The person reached the bottom of the steps and turned on the light in the shop. Kim could see the man in his slippers walking just near her. Kim held her breath. Her heart was pounding.

Suddenly, she heard a thud as the family cat came through the window and leaped to the floor. It curiously approached her and, with its white paws, started batting at the tassels on her sweatshirt.

"So, Kitty, what are you doing?" asked the man as he walked over to the bench.

Kim quickly pushed the tassels inside her shirt as the man stooped down to pick up the cat. "Why don't you come into my room tonight?" he said to the cat.

Purring, the cat nestled into the man's arms as he shuffled away towards the steps. He turned out the light in the shop, and Kim breathed a sigh of relief. She had never been so scared in her life.

Quickly, she crawled out from under the bench and darted to the window, squeezed through it, and fell to the ground among the bed of flowers. Sam was in the bushes and ran up to her.

"What happened in there?" he asked.

"I'm never doing anything like that again, Sam," she answered. "Let's go." The two teens ran through the dark streets back to Frau Grüber's. They crept inside the door and back into Kim's room.

"So, what did you see, Kimmy?" asked Sam.

CHAPTER EIGHT: MIRACLE IN A CHAPEL

"Alright, Sam. I'll tell you what I saw," said Kim. "There was an argument between Johannes, the brother of the young woman who stole the manuscript, and his father. The father wanted him and his sister Katrina to leave the house because of the stolen manuscript. In fact, the father said that Katrina had a curse on her. She was paralyzed because she stole it."

"So, where did they go when they were kicked out? Maybe that could lead us to the manuscript," said Sam.

"Johannes mentioned a town where there was a chapel. People were healed there, and he wanted to take his sister there."

"What was the name of the town, Kim?"

"It started with an S, I think. Oh, how could I forget it?"

"Don't worry. It'll come back to you."

"If I heard it again, I think I'd recognize it."

"You will. I'm sure of it. In the meantime, we have to tell your dad about what you experienced."

"Oh, no. I was dreading that. How are we going to tell him without also letting him know that we sneaked into the shop?"

"I guess we'll just have to tell him the truth," said Sam. "Don't worry, Kim, I'm also involved here, and I'll take responsibility for our decision."

"Okay, Sam. Let's tell him everything," said Kim. "I'm sure that we'll be punished, although being 'grounded' isn't really an option under these circumstances.

That morning, before breakfast, they knocked on Stride's door.

"Dad, we need to talk to you," said Kim.

"Sure, Kim, what's up?" Stride answered.

"We did something that you won't be happy about, but it was for a good cause," said Sam reluctantly. He was looking down at his shoes, so as not to look at Stride directly.

Stride looked at them, not sure how to respond.

"Well, tell me what it was, and I'll try to be as fair-minded as possible," he said with some foreboding.

"You remember how Mr. Jürgen wouldn't let us buy the cellist sculpture yesterday?" asked Kim.

"What about it?" answered Stride.

"I thought that if Kim could just touch the sculpture again, that it would reveal some valuable information about the manuscript," said Sam.

"That sounds reasonable," said Stride. "But certainly old man Jürgen wouldn't let us get near it again," he added.

"Exactly," said Sam. "So, I figured that we could sneak into the shop when everyone was asleep. Then Kim could touch it and let it reveal the information we needed. We would then leave without being noticed."

"Oh, no, you didn't. Did you?" asked Stride.

"Yes, we did. Sorry, Dad," said Kim, apologetically. "A window was open so I sort of ...slid in."

"Did anyone see you?" Stride asked. "Because if they did, you could get a stiff fine for illegal entry, you know. And it would be very bad for me if it got back to the University."

"No one saw us and we didn't get caught, so we're alright," said Kim.

"I certainly hope so, but I think we should get the first train out of town. Pack your bags, kids. I don't know how they deal with juvenile offenders in this country. Perhaps not as leniently as in the States," added Stride. After paying the bill, they caught the first train to Luzern. The trio looked very guilty, furtively glancing around until the train arrived and they hopped on. Just as the train wound around the lake, they saw a gleaming gold building on the top of a high mountain on the opposite shore. "Look up there," said Stride. "That's an old hotel called the Sonnenberg."

"What's the name of that town, Dad?" asked Kim.

"Seelisberg," answered Stride.

"That's it, Sam." cried Kim. "That's the name of the town I heard."

"Way to go!" said Sam.

"Well, Dad, I actually did have a vision when I held the sculpture. This town has a chapel where people get cured from being paralyzed. Can we go there?" asked Kim.

"And why would we want to go there?" asked Stride.

"I had better back up and start from the beginning," said Kim.

"Yes, please do. We were so concerned about getting out of town that I never did hear about your vision," said Stride.

"Well, Dad, when I held the sculpture, I again saw the man, Johannes, who received the manuscript from his sister, Katrina, the maid servant who stole it from the Schumanns. Their father was banishing him from his house and from town. He was accusing Johannes of putting a curse on the family, which resulted in Katrina being paralyzed as punishment for taking the manuscript. Johannes wanted to take Katrina to a healing chapel in Seelisberg to cure her," explained Kim.

"Well, I guess that makes sense," said Stride. "But it seems that this story is never ending."

"There's one thing that I don't understand, Dad," said Kim, looking up at the top of the mountain.

"What's that, Kim?"

"Who do you suppose created that beautiful sculpture of the cellist?" she asked.

"Well, it had to be done by a woodcarver, someone who knew about the manuscript and obviously appreciated the effect of the music on the musician playing it," said Stride. "Remember how blissful her face was? As if she were having a religious experience? I saw such a face on the statue of St. Theresa of Avila when she was pierced by divine love. It was the same sort of facial and bodily expression."

"Maybe more parts of this puzzle will fit together if we visit the chapel," said Sam.

"Alright," said Stride. "I guess Seelisberg is our next stop then."

After they got off the train in Luzern, they took a bus that wound its way up a steep mountain towards Seelisberg. When they arrived, Kim gasped. There was a sudden drop of hundreds of feet to the lake below.

"My gosh!" Kim exclaimed. "I wouldn't get too close to the edge of this cliff."

"Don't worry," replied Sam. "There's a guard rail to prevent you from falling off."

Then, Professor Stride said, "Did you know that Swiss independence from Austrian Hapsburg rule started right below here in a place called Rütli?"

"You mean Switzerland didn't exist as a country at that time?" asked Sam.

"No. It didn't. There were just isolated cantons or provinces. Three of them got together and drew up a declaration demanding their freedom," explained Stride.

"And that's how Switzerland became a country?" asked Kim.

"Yes," replied Stride. "Then, more provinces kept adding on, from the ones in the French-speaking west, to the Italian-speaking south and the German-speaking east. That's why Switzerland has three official languages."

It amazed Kim that her father even knew about Swiss history.

Finally, they found the little chapel. It didn't seem very imposing on the outside, but after they entered through a little porch in the back, they came into a rather large room. The altar in front was lit by candles and surrounded by sweet smelling roses, dahlias and peonies in vases. What was unusual, though, about this chapel was what could be seen on the walls. They were covered with crutches! Not only crutches, but also miniature paintings.

"What's all this about, Dad?" asked Kim. "I never saw anything so strange in my life."

"Yes, it's unusual, and a bit eerie when you first look at it," said Stride, "but, when you look at these paintings, you can see that they depict people being healed. These are the individual stories of the miracles that occurred in this chapel.

"And the crutches?" asked Sam.

"Well, these are the crutches that were no longer needed when the people were healed. They could just walk away without them," added Stride.

"Awesome!" exclaimed Sam.

Kim wandered around the chapel, as if drawn to something she didn't yet understand, until she came to one very small miniature painting. It depicted a woman who was being raised from the arms of a man and about to walk on her own. There was an inscription underneath in a flowery German script.

"Dad, can you read this?" asked Kim.

Stride and Sam walked over to where she was standing and looked at the painting and inscription. Stride translated, "In gratitude of the Lord's healing. Katrina and Johannes Jürgen,"

"So, she was healed here," said Sam. "I wonder what happened to them next? Kimmy, try touching the painting," he continued excitedly.

"Alright, Sam," said Kim. She touched the painting and felt a strange sensation in her arms, as if she were a sculptor carving something out of wood.

"That's it," she cried. "Johannes was the sculptor and he did it out of gratitude for his sister's healing."

"But the sculpture was of a cellist. Doesn't that have something to do with the manuscript?" asked Sam.

"You're right, Sam," answered Stride. "There's some connection that we're missing. Maybe the sculpture is telling us about what they did with the manuscript."

"Sorry, guys," said Kim. "I'm not getting any more out of this painting. Let's go outside. I'm feeling a bit claustrophobic in here."

"Yeah, me too," said Sam.

As they left the chapel, with only part of the Jürgen mystery solved, they noticed a beautiful flower garden with the same flowers that were placed on the altar. A very old woman was bent over, lovingly tending the flowers. Her fluffy white cat sat by her side, focused on a bug that was crawling on the ground.

"Dad, maybe she knows something about the painting," said Kim. "Why don't you ask her?"

"You're right, Kim," said Stride. "She looks like the caretaker of this little chapel."

Stride carefully walked over to the edge of the garden and asked her in German, "My dear woman, good afternoon. Could you please tell me something about one of the paintings in the chapel?"

She answered in the Swiss German that he was beginning to understand.

"Good afternoon, kind sir. There are so many paintings that I don't know the ones painted before my time."

"This one has the inscription with the names of Katrina and Johannes Jürgen," he said.

"Yes, I remember that one well. Those young people were so grateful that they joined the local monks and nuns, devoting their lives to God."

"And, do you remember anything about an old manuscript or a woodcarving of a cellist?"

"Ah, let me think. Yes, it was a long while ago, of course, and I was just a girl at the time, daughter of the caretaker here. What was it you asked about? A manuscript? And a woodcarving?" she asked.

"Yes," said Stride. "If you know anything about them, I'd be most grateful for whatever you could tell me."

"Please, come inside with your young ones and have a cup of tea," she said distractedly, as if still racking her brain about those items.

They followed her into the house, which was so antique that it seemed to bow in the direction of the lake. The door was covered with moss and lichen, and flowers surrounded the outer walls so that the little house seemed part of the earth. Inside was dark, with only small windows letting in the daylight. Kim had never been inside such an ancient house and was thoroughly charmed by every item she saw, from the mossy wooden bucket to the white billowing curtains on the windows.

The old woman showed them to chairs around a small dining table and put up water for tea on an old wood stove. She brought out earthenware cups with chamomile leaves in a small bowl. Watching her, Kim felt transported in time. She looked out the small windows to see the mountain peaks surrounding the lake. They were up so high that the air was thin. Her head felt light and airy as a vision came to her of figures who were here in this house in a previous time. *She saw Johannes and Katrina Jürgen giving a manuscript to a man dressed in brown robes. In the corner, she saw a young child looking on. The people were talking in low voices.*

"Brüder Martin," said Johannes, "I am grateful that you accept me into your fold as a monk, as is my sister. In gratitude, we want to donate this old manuscript to the church."

"You need not give the church anything, just your love and devotion, but we accept it graciously and will take good care of it," Brüder Martin said.

The child looked on in wonderment as her mother brought in a tray of tea and home baked cookies for the religious group. There was barely enough room in the little house for so many people, but the mother said, "Ada, please get me your little stool, the one with the roses painted on it, so that we have a seat for everyone." The child promptly ran up some stairs and came down with her small stool, placing it cautiously near the woman who was to become a nun.

"I must make a confession to you of a sin I have committed in relation to this manuscript, however," continued Johannes. "My sister took it from a family

when she worked there as a maid. When my father found out, he banished both of us. I also was guilty of accepting it and trying to sell it. We now realize that this sin affected my sister so badly that she became paralyzed. When we were banished, I took her to this chapel to heal her. We are both so grateful to see the Lord's work that we wish to give our lives to Him."

"But, do you not wish to make amends with your father in some way?" asked Brüder Martin. "Our way is one of forgiveness and love, you know".

Johannes looked ashamed, not knowing what to say.

"As for the manuscript, after what you have told me, we need to give it back to its rightful owners," Brüder Martin added. "We cannot keep stolen property."

"Yes, you are right, Brüder Martin," added Johannes. "Unfortunately, the rightful owner has passed away, and it's been a number of years since we've had contact with the rest of the family."

"Well," said Brüder Martin, "we will keep the manuscript safely in our vaults and try to find the heirs. This terrible War that is raging makes it impossible, of course, to attend to that now, but should we not succeed, we will accept it as an offering to the Church."

"As you know," explained Johannes, "I was trained as a skilled woodcarver. This manuscript is for a cellist. I have sung the melody myself, since I know a little music, and it is heavenly inspired. I will carve something that shows the beauty of the music and its effect on anyone who listens to it. I will send that to my father."

At this point, the vision slowly faded. Kim felt sad to lose it. As she focused on the mountain peaks outside the window, she was brought back again to the present scene with her father, Sam and the old woman, who, she now realized, was the little girl named Ada in her vision.

"I am trying to remember the items you are talking about, but nothing comes back to me," the old woman said.

"Dad, ask her about a little stool painted with roses," said Kim.

Now, completely confident in Kim's suggestions, Stride asked the woman, "Do you remember anything about a little stool painted with flowers?"

"Ah, yes, I remember. It was in my mother's house for many years," Ada replied. Then she looked uncertain. "But I don't remember anything about a woodcarving."

"That's alright. You have given us much good information. Thank you so very much," replied Stride.

They walked out of the crumbling, yet charming old house and saw that a haze had formed over the lake. When they looked out at the mountain range, it seemed as if a sea of clouds raised the lake up in front of them.

"Dad, this place certainly looks like miracles would take place here," said Kim. "Does the name Seelisberg mean anything in particular? It seems every name has a hidden meaning in this country."

"Well, let me guess," said Stride. "I know that 'Seele' in German means 'soul' and 'Berg' means 'mountain,' so Seelisberg could mean 'soul' or 'holy' mountain."

"Does that get us any closer to finding the manuscript?" asked Sam, bringing them both back into focus. "Kim, I noticed that you were having a vision for a bit in there. What did you see, and how did you know to ask about the footstool? What did her answer mean? Please fill us in."

"There's a restaurant next door, which I can tell you is called the 'Waldhaus' or 'forest house' since you both love to know the meaning of names," said Stride. "Let's go there for our supper, let Kim tell us what she saw, and think over our next moves."

Seelisberg

"Spoken like a true detective, Dad," added Kim.

They sat down at a table on an outdoor balcony overlooking the mountain range and ordered "fitness salads." When their dishes arrived, they reviewed the day's events.

"So tell us, Kim, what happened to you in there?" asked Sam again.

"Well, from what I could gather, the Jürgens joined a religious order out of gratitude for Katrina's healing. There was a Brüder Martin to whom they gave the manuscript, but Johannes told him it was stolen. Then, the monk wanted to give it back to the rightful owners but couldn't because of some War."

"That was probably World War I," said Stride.

"And what about the cellist carving?"

"The monk said that Johannes should make peace with his family, so Johannes said he would make a woodcarving that would show the beauty of the music and the effect it had on anyone who listened to it. He was going to have it presented to his father," said Kim. "Oh, I noticed one more thing. The old lady was a young child named Ada who brought that flowered foot stool for Katrina Jürgen to sit on."

"So, now we know what happened to the Jürgens and why the family would not sell the woodcarving of the cellist. What we don't know is where the manuscript is now. How are we going to find that out?" asked Stride.

"I haven't figured that out, yet," said Kim, uncertainly.

"Well, I think that whenever we've felt that we have reached a dead-end, with no further clues to go on, we had to rely on you to get us back on track," said Stride. "Remember when that happened in Nyon? Then, you felt drawn to the Alps and that got us back on track again."

"So, Dad, what are you saying? It's up to me as to where we go next?" asked Kim.

"I don't want to put you on the spot, Kim," said Stride. "Suppose we just go back to Luzern, stay there overnight, and plan on going back to Salzburg, unless something else happens along the way?"

"That sounds good, Dad. It's not like I can call upon these visions whenever I wish. They just 'happen' to me," said Kim.

"Yes, your mother said that to me once as well," answered Stride wistfully.

They went back down to Luzern, taking the boat instead of the train so they could enjoy the water and the view of the circle of mountains around the lake. Arriving in Luzern, they found a bed and breakfast and were eager to enjoy a night's sleep. Kim drifted off, having pleasant visions of roses and water. Then, towards early morning, she heard a strange noise. Someone was in her room!

CHAPTER NINE: A MONASTERY SECRET

"Who's there?" Kim demanded, as she turned on the lamp by her bed. A figure could be seen leaving through the balcony where the door had been left open. Jumping out of bed, she banged on her father's door. He opened it anxiously.

"Oh, Dad," she cried. "Someone was in my room and jumped over the balcony when I surprised him." Kim was trembling.

"Don't worry, Kim, it's all right now," he said, taking her in his arms to calm her. Then, Sam appeared at the door.

"What's going on?" he asked.

"Someone was in her room," explained Stride.

"This is really spooky," said Sam. "Why would anyone want to bother Kim?"

"Maybe they are really after me," said Stride. "Remember those two men who were following us in the Alps and in Vienna? I'm sure it has something to do with the manuscript."

Kim was recovering now and remembered something.

"Dad, last night I was dreaming. It was something about water and roses, of all things," she said. "Robed figures were tending these roses."

"What kind of robes, Kim?" asked Stride. "Were they like monks?"

"Yes, now that you mention it," she replied. "What

made you think of that?"

"Well, your earlier vision with Johannes and Brüder Martin involved a monk. And, we know that the manuscript was in the hands of the monastery when Jürgen gave it to them. So, we need to find out which monastery had the manuscript. It seems unlikely that it found its way back to the Schumanns because there would have been some record of it in the family, and it certainly would have been published. That's why we need to find that monastery," said Stride.

"So, what does water and roses make you think of, sir?" asked Sam.

"Well, what comes to mind is a place I once visited on the lake around Zürich. It's a town called Rapperswil, also known as the 'City of Roses' because the monks take care of the many rose gardens there," answered Stride.

"I guess that's our next stop. How do we get there, Dad?" asked Kim.

"We have to go to Zürich first and then take a local train. It's almost morning already, so why don't we pack our bags, pay the bill, and go to the Luzern train station? We can get our breakfast along the way," he replied.

While waiting at the train station, Kim and Sam kept looking around to make sure that they weren't being followed. They were getting especially wary of anyone who was possibly trying to stop them from finding the manuscript. *That must have been the reason why someone broke into my room,* Kim thought.

Finally, their train arrived and they boarded quickly to find an empty compartment for their trip to Zürich. When they arrived, the Zürich station seemed vast and confusing, but they finally found their way to the local train to Rapperswil, a town overlooking Lake

76

Zürich with a distant view of the Alps. From there, Stride asked for the local monastery.

When they arrived, they were led into a courtyard, beautifully tended by monks who were planting roses. Ushered by one of the monks into a small stone room that was very sparsely decorated with a crucifix and small wall hangings, they sat on ancient wood-carved chairs. A few moments later, an elderly, kind-looking monk entered. He gave each of his guests a polite smile, sat down at his desk, and introduced himself as Father Schmidt.

"What can I do for you?" he asked.

"We are here on an unusual errand," said Stride, "to find a lost manuscript. I have been sent by my university in the U.S. to evaluate it and buy it for our music collection."

"What sort of manuscript?" asked the monk.

"It's a cello concerto of Mozart. Apparently, it was given to the church by a man named Johannes Jürgen when he joined the order, quite a long time ago, in the early 1900's."

"Actually," replied Father Schmidt, "I recall hearing about something like that a long time ago from one of the monks, a Brüder Martin who died at an advanced age many years ago. He told me that it was kept in a vault here because the owners could not be found. The manuscript was received at the beginning of the First World War, and there was so much confusion in those days. Then, it was sold to a music collector named Aaron Strauss in order to raise funds for charity. After that, I have no idea what happened to it, what with the Nazi appropriation of Jewish art objects."

"Do you have any idea what happened to Aaron Strauss?" asked Stride.

"Well, as you know, many of these unfortunate

people were sent to the gas chambers. We hid some of them here until after the Second World War. In fact, if I check my records, I know that one of them was sheltered here as a favor to this same Herr Strauss."

Father Schmidt then went to a filing cabinet and riffled through some yellowed papers. While he was searching among these old documents, Kim detected a presence in the little stone room. *She felt as if she were floating back in time and saw two figures; one was an older, bearded man with glasses and the other was a young boy. As she focused more deeply, she heard sounds of weeping from the boy and soft, comforting speech from the father of the boy. "Don't worry, my dear Abel, they will take good care of you here."*

"But I don't want you to leave, Papa," cried the boy. "How long do I have to stay?"

"Just until after the War. Then, I will come for you. I promise," said the father, fighting back tears himself.

"How will you be safe? Won't they hurt you when they know who you are?" pleaded the boy.

"I must go back. I have to run the business and take care of your mother, your grandmother and your sister, Marta," he replied. "They cannot vanish as easily as you, my dear son."

"Whatever you say, Papa," said the boy tearfully.

"One last thing, my son," he continued, "I want you to take care of something, a manuscript. Hide it well in your room, and when you leave, take it with you. It is very valuable. It is a lost cello concerto by Mozart. I bought it recently from this monastery and was going to have it known to the world. But, with the Nazis everywhere now, I do not want this wonderful work to wind up in their brutal hands. If something should happen to me, you can sell it to have money to live on. Will you promise me that?"

"Of course, Papa. I will do anything you say. Please don't let anything happen to our family," said the boy.

"Don't worry, my son. I will do all that I can. Now, the monks will take good care of you here," said the father. Then, the scene faded. Kim returned to the present.

"Ah, yes," she heard Father Schmidt saying. "Of course we did not keep records with the original names because that would have been too dangerous. However, one person — a young man — was Strauss' son. Here it is. His name, Abel Strauss, was changed to Anton Starker. We kept the same initials, A.S." he said. "It seems that after the War, he went to study in Salzburg. However, we still don't know what happened to the manuscript."

"Thank you so much. This really helps," said Stride.

"I am glad to be of assistance. I hope that you find it. Think what a blessing it would be to discover some lost piece of music composed by our genius, Mozart," said the monk, showing them out into the courtyard and accompanying them to the gate.

Once outside, Kim was very excited.

"Dad, I saw Strauss and his son, there, in the room. He handed the manuscript over to his son," said Kim. "He gave him instructions to sell it so he could live off the money if he were alone in the world," said Kim.

"Well, then, that decides it! He must have taken it with him to Salzburg. Let's go back there and see if we can pick up the scent again," said Stride.

On the train back to Salzburg, the adventurers reviewed all they knew so far about the manuscript. After tracing it from Vienna to Venice, to Frau Mathilde Groschen in Nyon, to the Schumanns in the

Interlaken region, to the Jürgens in Brienz, to the monastery in Rapperswil, and now back to Salzburg, a number of inconsistencies still remained in Kim's mind.

"Dad, we still don't know if there was a copy from the original and whether the original or the copy was sent to Venice. Are there two manuscripts or just one? I'm confused," said Kim.

"You're right, Kim, it is confusing," answered Stride. "But, this is the way I figure it. The original was probably given to Claudia in that fire. Maybe the copy was sent to the cousin, Mathilde, in Venice, who passed it on to her family, Frau Mathilde, whom we met in Nyon. The original, however, seems to have been passed on from Claudia to her daughter, also named Claudia, who took lessons from Clara Schumann. This original was then stolen by the Jürgens, who gave it to the church. The church intended to give it back, but due to the War, they still had it in the vault and sold it to Aaron Strauss. During the Nazi regime, he gave it to his son Abel Strauss, who returned to Salzburg with it. So, there are indeed two manuscripts. Does this all make sense so far?" asked Stride.

"Yes, Dad, it seems to fit together," said Kim.

"I have just one question, sir," said Sam.

"What's that, Sam?"

"Well, sir, Salzburg is a pretty big town. Where do we find the manuscript?"

"That's a good point, Sam," said Stride. "What do you suggest?"

"I think that we should rely on Kim. Maybe make her walk through the city, like following one of those witching rods that tell you where water is, and see what sends her visions," answered Sam.

"Hey, guys, that puts a lot of pressure on me. You

know that I have to let things come to me. I can't control this," said Kim.

"Well, maybe it's time to learn to focus it when you need to," said Stride.

"What do you mean, Dad?" asked Kim.

"Remember how I told you that your mother had this same talent that you have?" said Stride. "Well, she learned that she could start focusing her ability to work for her when she really needed it."

"Is it sort of like when you give a dog a piece of clothing belonging to someone who's missing. Once the dog has the scent, he finds the person?" asked Sam.

"Well, woof woof to you, Sam!" said Kim, who was a little insulted. She didn't like the idea of being compared to a beagle.

"So, what do we know of Abel Strauss?" asked Kim.

"I'm not really sure, Kim," said Stride. "Maybe we need to find records of his life in Salzburg. Maybe he went to the university or conservatory there and lived somewhere nearby. We can ask for his name on school records around the mid-to-late 1940s, after the War. If they have an address for him, we can go there and ask around. What do you think?" asked Stride.

"Yes, that's good," said Sam.

Now, they were satisfied and could sit back and enjoy the rest of the trip. They got the distinct feeling, however, that they were being watched. As a man passed their compartment window, they saw him cast some furtive glances at them. This was not one of the two men they had seen before. This man was younger, blond and very shifty-looking.

"Dad, don't look now, but that man is spying on us," said Kim.

"Yeah," said Sam. "Maybe he's even the one who

broke into your room, Kim," said Sam. "That balcony was pretty high up, too high for one of those older guys we saw huffing and puffing up the mountain after us."

"Why would someone be so interested in following us, Dad?" asked Kim.

"I'm sure it has to do with our search for the manuscript. Someone is trying to find out if we're getting close to discovering where it is. As yet, I don't really know why. I guess we'll find out in time," he said.

At that moment, the train pulled into the Salzburg station. They took the bus back to their rented rooms at Frau Huber's. It felt good to be back after a week of traveling, even though they enjoyed seeing Italy and Switzerland in the process. Kim and Sam told their friend Heidi all about the places they visited and the things they did, but they did not mention the manuscript.

CHAPTER TEN: THE FORGOTTEN CELLO

The next morning, riding their bikes through the back meadows on their way to Salzburg, Kim and Sam looked up as the clouds rose above Untersberg, the huge mountain where they still wanted to go climbing before their stay ended.

"Do you see that little cable car that goes up there to the top?" asked Kim.

"Yup, and that would be quite a drop if the cable ever broke," replied Sam.

"Well, if you're afraid of cable cars, we can always climb up there," said Stride.

"Have you ever done that, Dad?" asked Kim.

"Yes, many times, in fact. There's a little wooden hut near the top where you can get drinks. In my student days, we had glüwine, which was wine with a little whiskey called 'schnapps' in it," said Stride. "It warmed you right up."

"I'll bet," said Sam. "If you're tipsy, you can come tumbling down the mountain pretty easily."

"Don't worry. We never got really drunk," said Stride.

When they reached town, they decided to head first to the Mozarteum. Finding the office of admissions, they were then sent to the records department for the documents dating back to students who were enrolled just after World War II. They asked for both names: Abel Strauss and Anton Starker, just in case Strauss had kept this false name to avoid anti-Semitism. They found that he had been enrolled as Abel Strauss from 1947 through 1949, majoring in cello and music history. They also found out that he had lived at Schloss Frohnburg, the international student house where Stride had lived. But, there was no further record beyond that. No forwarding address, no future known whereabouts.

As they were leaving the Mozarteum, Kim asked, "Dad, can we see one of the practice rooms while we're here?"

"Sure Kim. In fact, I will show you where I used to practice," said Stride. Then, they proceeded to wander among the rooms where all the different sounds were clanging against each other. One room was empty, and Kim walked into it as if it were a holy place. She could feel the presence of students who had practiced there for many hours, preparing for careers as musicians.

After a while, she said, "Okay, Dad. We can leave now."

"Let's go to the Frohnburg," said Stride. "I know that place well, as I lived there for two years. In fact, I never told you this before, but it was where I met your mother. We were both music students from the U.S."

"Wow, Dad! You met Mom here? That's incredible!" exclaimed Kim, suddenly aware of a chapter in her parents' lives she had never suspected.

"Yes, we were known as quite a romantic couple, Daniel and Gisella," Stride said, nostalgically.

"Isn't Gisella a German name?" asked Sam.

"Yes, she was born in the U.S., but her parents were German immigrants," said Stride. "They came over after the war, and Gisella always wanted to know her German roots. She found out that her grandmother was named Greta, but that's all she knew. War records were destroyed, so she couldn't find much beyond that."

"Dad, do you think that she still had family in Europe? Maybe I'm related to someone over here?" asked Kim.

"That's very possible, Kim," answered Stride. "But, we have no way of knowing. Anyway, we have enough of a mystery to solve with the manuscript."

They rode their bikes through the back meadows, passing little chapels along the way where people could meditate next to a wooden carved crucifix. Under the constant, imposing shadow of the Untersberg in front of them, they reached Helbrunner Alleé, covered with graceful, towering trees providing shade and coolness. Halfway down the Alleé, they reached the Frohnburg. Placing their bikes on the racks, they opened the huge, heavy wooden doors, entering into the vast hallway covered in stone slabs. It was noticeably cooler inside. They went to the house father's desk and inquired about the student, Abel Strauss, who had lived there quite a long time ago. Herr Mannheim was very cordial and told them in very good English that he didn't know the student, but definitely knew about him.

"How come?' asked Kim.

"Because of his cello," replied Herr Mannheim.

"His cello?" asked Sam.

"Yes, his cello was left here and has been used by students for recitals when their own cellos were not a good enough quality," replied Herr Mannheim.

"May we please see the cello?" asked Stride.

"Yes, of course. I keep it locked up in my office. Please come this way," invited Herr Mannheim. He grabbed some keys off the wall and unlocked his office in a room behind his desk. As they walked in, piles of papers and books stacked everywhere, they glimpsed the cello case lying beside the far wall.

"Do you play the cello?" asked Mannheim.

"No, not really, but may my daughter just touch it? I am encouraging her to take up cello and this might inspire her," said Stride.

"Well, of course. I am always happy to see a potential music student," said Mannheim. "Take as much time as you like while I deal with some business matters," he added as he walked out of the room.

Kim went over to the cello case, opened it and touched the soft, brown wood. She ran her fingers along the strings and let her hands follow the gentle curves of the body. *Closing her eyes, she could feel something of the original owner's gentleness and love for the instrument. Abel was a good-hearted young man with high ideals about family honor and devotion to their memory. She could feel that through touching his cello. But she also felt something else, as if there were some real connection between the two of them.*

Finally, she said, "Alright, Dad. We can go now." Stride and Sam looked at her expectantly.

Then, she realized what they were hoping for and said, "No, no visions. At least, not yet. But I could feel the presence of this sweet man. Come on, let's go," she said, almost in tears, although she didn't know why she should feel so sad.

"Thank you, Herr Mannheim," said Stride. "We are grateful to you for showing us the Strauss cello."

"Oh, it is my pleasure," answered Mannheim.

As they were leaving, Stride had one more question. "By the way, do you know what happened to

Hellbrunner Allee

Abel Strauss?"

"Not really. I only heard that one day he mysteriously disappeared. They never could find a trace of him. That's all I know," said Mannheim.

That evening, the three adventurers decided on a chicken dinner at the restaurant where Stride went on Sundays as a student. Only cold- cuts were served for dinner at the Frohnburg. It used to be the cook's day off. All the students who could afford it would have a wonderful dinner at the local restaurant, instead.

During their meal, Kim asked, "Dad, if you lived in the Frohnburg, how come you didn't know about Strauss' cello?"

"That's a good question, Kim," replied Stride. "Actually, we knew of a cello being kept in the office, but no one ever asked to play it or inquired about the owner. Somehow, that was kept secret, and I don't know why. Maybe they were hoping for the original owner to come back and claim it."

When dinner ended, they decided to turn in early and cycled back to their rooms.

After they went to bed that night, Kim began to think of what her father had said about focusing her thoughts in order to find out more about the missing manuscript. *She began to drift to sleep. Suddenly, she saw a bright light above her, even though she knew the room was dark. It was the light from the chandelier in one of the practice rooms she'd seen in the Mozarteum they'd visited that day. Softly, and then louder, she heard the sounds of two cellos playing one of the Bach unaccompanied cello suites. She was able to distinguish the voices and saw the faces of two young men, bent over their cellos, playing this beautifully calm music.*

"Abel," said the older-looking student, stopping and turning to his companion. "What is that secret you said you were going to tell me about some family treasure you've managed to keep hidden all this time?"

Kim quickly drew in a breath of surprise. Although many years younger than he was now, she couldn't be mistaken. This older man was none other than Hauser, the manuscript collector who had told them of the disappearance of the concerto!

The younger of the two stopped playing and looked a little startled. "I'll tell you about it this evening,

Hans. I've decided to reveal what I have to the administration at the Conservatory, but I wanted you to be the first to know about it. You have been my one true friend here. The other students only pretend that my being a Jew makes no difference to them."

"Well," said Hans, "it makes no difference to me. You are a good musician. But, what is this secret about?"

"As I said," replied Abel, "I'll tell you this evening."

Kim stirred in bed, and the scene in her vision shifted to a comfortable room that had two beds and walls lined with book shelves. The shelves were filled with music manuscripts and books about musicians. The two cellos that she'd seen in her previous vision were now resting against a wall. The roommates were sitting beside each other at a desk, each smoking a pipe and dressed in bathrobes.

"Finally," said Hans, "you can show me this family treasure you have been hiding. Is it, by any chance, some musical marvel?" he added, laughing.

"It is far more than that, Hans," said Abel. "It is a treasure beyond price." With those words, he unlocked a drawer in the desk and carefully removed wrapped pieces of parchment, the kind of paper that was used for writing music hundreds of years ago. "Just look at that, Hans!" Abel said with a smile, handing the manuscript to his friend.

The older student peered at the manuscript and read the first measures. Then, his jaw fell.

"Is this authentic? It is clearly in the style of Mozart, but I've never heard that he wrote a cello concerto," he asked, barely speaking above a whisper.

Abel merely nodded, and somehow Kim, in her vision, could see the title page of the manuscript and the first pages as Hans delicately leafed through it. It

*was the same manuscript that she had seen in her
first vision. It was the Mozart cello concerto!*

*"Is this the only copy?" asked Hans, his voice still
weak from astonishment.*

*"It isn't a copy, Hans. It's the original! That is, as
far as I have been able to determine. Of course, until
some expert comes to authenticate it, we can't be
absolutely sure."*

*"My father bought it from an old monastery, the
very place where I was hidden during the War. He
told me to keep it for the sake of the family, but, as
you know, I am intending to go to Palestine once my
studies are done here at the end of the term. I would
have taken it with me, but, in spite of what terrible
things have been done to my people, I believe that
this great work should stay in Salzburg, the town of
Mozart's birth. It would be best cared for here and
then published, so that all the world's cellists can
enjoy a new addition to their repertoire."*

*"But, this is a priceless work!" exclaimed Hans,
amazed at his friend's intentions. "You could get a
fortune for it!"*

*"I guess so, but I feel that it would do greater
honor to my family if it were known that the Strauss
family donated the original manuscript of the Mozart
cello concerto to the town of his birth. I think that if I
accepted money for it, it would not be right," Abel
explained.*

*"And, when do you intend to donate it to the
Conservatory?" said Hans, with concern in his voice.*

*"At the end of the term, in two weeks. I just
wanted to share this moment with you before the
announcement is made. If you'd like, you can sight-
read it now," said Abel.*

*Trembling, Hans placed the manuscript on a
music stand, and picked up his cello. He then sat*

down and began to play the beautiful work. Kim heard the sounds, and again it seemed to her to be one of the loveliest things she'd ever heard. In her vision, tears began to stream down Hans' face with the pure joy of playing the music. Abel smiled proudly as his friend played through the whole concerto, almost flawlessly.

Then Kim awoke. It was morning. She still didn't know what had become of the concerto manuscript, but now she was sure that Hauser had something to do with it. If only she could find out what that something was!

CHAPTER ELEVEN: MOUNTAIN REVELATION

The next day, Stride, Kim and Sam decided to climb the Untersberg. The weather was perfect, sunny and clear, yet not too hot for strenuous climbing. Even Heidi went with them this time, having received permission from her mother to accompany them. She knew the area very well and could show them many hidden landmarks, like a real castle with a moat, on their way to the Untersberg.

After hours of climbing almost to the top of the mountain, Stride was true to his word and took them to the little wooden hut where he had gone as a student. As they entered the small building, Kim was totally charmed by the view through the small wooden windows. She could see the distant valley far below and the speck of the cable car slowly climbing towards the summit. "I sure am glad we climbed instead of taking that cable car," said Sam. "Imagine if that thing broke! The people would plunge to their death."

"Now don't get yourself all worked up, Sam," said Kim. "I'm sure that there has never been a fall with that thing, right dad?"

"Not that I know of," replied Stride. "What do you

think, Heidi?"

"I have not heard of the cable car breaking, ever," she replied.

The teens ordered hot chocolate with whipped cream. Stride had his glüwein.

"Don't get too drunk, dad," said Kim. "I don't think we can get you down the mountain, unless you can fly down," she teased.

They heard little tinkling bells from goats grazing on the steep hillside outside the hut. The air was very thin at this elevation, and having enjoyed their rest, the foursome followed a path around the mountain with its ever-changing views.

Finally, when the afternoon sun was beginning to lower in the sky, they decided to hike down past shrubby trees, blown by the wind and stunted in their growth. Slowly, they felt the air becoming fuller as they descended into the valley.

"Heidi, do you go hiking in the mountains often?" asked Sam.

"Oh, yes, we go with my school group, especially in the nice spring weather," she said, her long blond braids beginning to come undone from getting caught in tree branches.

Finally, reaching the bottom and biking back to their chalet, they all felt quite exhausted from the day's adventure. Kim hadn't yet told her dad about the vision of Hans and Abel that she had the previous night because there was so much that she didn't understand yet. She needed to sift it through her mind.

That night, no sooner had Kim fallen asleep, than she had another vision. This came from the image she had of the beautiful view from the top of the mountain that they had climbed that afternoon. But, now she saw Hans and Abel climbing this mountain. She didn't hear their voices at first, but Hans' voice eventually became clear to her.

"You're a fool, Abel! You should reconsider what you're doing if you just give up the manuscript like this. If it were mine, I'd make sure to secure a good price for it before I revealed its existence. That way, you could..."

"I told you that is out of the question, Hans!" Abel replied sharply. "It will be a memorial to my family if it's donated. I owe it to my poor parents and sister to do this! Now, let's not talk about it anymore. I thought you'd enjoy the sight from here before we leave this place after graduation tomorrow. I have asked to meet with the Director then to present the manuscript. It will be quite a surprise. Aside from the two of us, no one knows of its existence yet."

They were walking along the edge of a huge cliff that looked out over the city. Salzburg, from Kim's vision, looked like a magical town right out of a fairytale. At that moment, she heard a cry that almost woke her. It was Abel, falling from the cliff down to the ground below. Hans, with a big smile on his face, was watching the impending death of his friend!

Kim woke with a shriek! She had witnessed a murder, but how could she ever prove it had happened? Doubtless, Hans Hauser would have reported that his dear friend, Abel Strauss, had met with "an unfortunate accident." And, now she knew that they were not just dealing with a thief, but a murderer!

Kim couldn't sleep for the rest of the night. She found herself weeping uncontrollably over the tragic fate of young Abel. Remembering the vibrations of the gentleness she had received from touching his cello, she mourned the loss of such a beautiful person.

Towards morning, she told her father and Sam that she had to talk with them. Stride, feeling a bit achy from hiking all day, said sleepily, "Alright Kim. Let's meet on the balcony."

The balcony faced Untersberg, where they'd hiked the previous day. It stood, majestic in the morning light. But, Kim found it ominous. All their jokes about cable cars breaking suddenly depressed her.

"I've got to tell you about my last two visions, Dad," she said.

Stride, sitting uncomfortably in the chair, said "I'm listening, Kim." Sam looked a bit more excited and expectant.

"Well, to start with, we have more than a thief on our hands. It turns out that Abel Strauss was murdered," she said.

Stride suddenly looked up in surprise. "You saw someone murder him?" he asked.

"He was pushed off a big cliff, the one on Untersberg," Kim answered. They looked up at the mountain now, with a mix of astonishment and fear.

"Who did it?" asked Sam.

"Our friendly manuscript dealer, Hauser!" she replied. "He and Abel were music students together at the conservatory, and Abel revealed that he was going to donate the original manuscript to the conservatory."

"So, he did have the original!" exclaimed Stride.

"But, why would Hauser want to kill Abel?" asked Sam.

"To keep the manuscript for himself, of course. He's also a cellist, you know," said Kim.

"But, he said it was lost or stolen from his vault," said Sam.

"I suppose that was to throw us off track," said Stride.

"So Karl Hess' suspicions about Hauser were

right all along," said Kim. "But why wouldn't Hauser want us to buy it?"

"I haven't figured that out yet, Kim," said her father. "But, before we make any accusations about Hauser's involvement in Abel's death, we need to find proof."

"Do you think that after all these years, there would be some proof up on the mountain?" asked Sam.

"Well, maybe not UP on the mountain, but maybe DOWN where Kim saw Abel fall, beneath the big cliff," answered Stride.

"Why don't we go there, Dad, and look around?"

Stride, already aching from the previous day's adventure, reluctantly agreed. "Yes, I suppose, as long as we don't do too much climbing. I don't think I could lift my legs even two inches without hurting."

After breakfast, the trio rode their bikes to the foot of the mountain, below the big cliff where Kim saw Abel fall in her vision. They rummaged among the rocks and trees without success and were about to give up trying, when suddenly Sam called out, "Look what I found!"

Sure enough, something shiny was gleaming in the bushes. Picking it up, Sam saw that it was a cuff link, gritty with dirt and pine needles. On the outside were the initials H.H.

"Who could that be, sir?" Sam asked Stride.

"Ah, that's surely the devious Hans Hauser, don't you think? This may be the proof we need, Sam."

"But, why aren't there any signs of Abel? Do you think he was found and led away? Or, if he died here, wouldn't his bones be left, even after all these years?" asked Kim.

"I really don't know, Kim. Let's just take this home and think about what to do next," said Stride.

CHAPTER TWELVE: CAUGHT IN THE ACT

On their way home from the Untersberg, Stride sensed that someone was following him. Every time they made a turn, he noticed that the other person did so as well. Finally, he determined that they were being followed. It occurred to him that, since they knew something about Hauser, he had sent someone to follow them and maybe even try to stop them from learning more.

Stride had an idea, saying to Kim and Sam who were peddling behind him, "Follow me. I'm going to do some tricky biking now."

Sam and Kim looked at each other as if understanding that something suspicious was happening and nodded to Stride. Then, Stride took a quick turn behind a chalet, followed by Sam and Kim. Since they were out of sight of their pursuer at that point, they kept an eye out as he rode by. Then, they started following him!

Just as the man was about to ride into Hellbrunner Alleé, he must have realized that he lost the trio, so he took a side road back towards Salzburg. The trio followed him, keeping a safe distance.

"That's the blond guy we saw on the train," realized Kim.

Then, the man stopped at a small chalet at the edge of town, right by the mountain leading up to Hohensalzburg, the medieval fortress overlooking the town. The fortress protected the town in earlier times. He parked his bike in an old stand and went inside, leaving the door slightly ajar.

Stride and the two friends parked their bikes behind an old tree and quietly walked up to the door. There was no one immediately inside, so they tiptoed cautiously into the hallway, being careful not to make a sound. Hearing voices coming from a nearby room, they crouched down beside the slightly opened door and heard, as Stride suspected, the hired detective talking to Hauser. Since they were talking in German, only Stride could understand what they were saying.

"I tried to follow them, but when I got to the Alleé, I just lost their trail," said the man. "So, I turned around and came back here."

"That was not smart, Heinrich," said Hauser. "Don't you realize that they could have followed you instead? I can't let Stride know where I live. And, those brats of his seem to be one step ahead of us."

"I can get back on the job tomorrow, if you like," said Heinrich.

"Yes, please do, and report back to me every detail. I am coming close to selling something rather important, and I can't afford to have Stride mess things up for me," said Hauser.

Heinrich made signs of leaving, so the trio hid behind a staircase until he was gone. Then, Stride grabbed his chance. He saw Hauser looking toward the window and slipped into the room. Hauser, hearing a noise behind him, turned around startled.

"What are you doing here, Professor Stride? I don't remember inviting you," said Hauser very coolly.

"No, I don't think that you would exactly invite me here, Herr Hauser, especially when you have those two manuscripts to hide from me," answered Stride. Sure enough, on Hauser's desk were two old parchment music scores. One was certainly the original Mozart cello concerto, and the other was the copy!

"Everything was going as planned until you came here with your meddling, Professor Stride," Hauser said, visibly shaken that Stride had seen the two manuscripts on the table.

"I don't understand," said Stride goading him on, "After all, you sent for me, didn't you?"

"My assistant, Hess, your old friend, wrote to you before I could stop him! I couldn't let him know that I didn't want you here," he continued. "You see," he said a little hesitantly touching one of the manuscripts, "I couldn't take a chance that the one you were supposed to identify, the one Mrs. Groschen sent me, was the authentic Mozart manuscript. Then, you'd let the University know, and I would have had to give most of the proceeds to her."

"But if her manuscript had been the copy...?" Stride asked.

"Then, you would have bought it for the University. And, I would know that I had the original to sell to a wealthy buyer interested in it. You see, I was no longer sure which was the copy, and I couldn't take a chance that you would identify Groschen's as the original; that discovery would have cost me millions!"

"But, haven't you had it all these years?" asked Kim. "Why didn't you ever try to sell it before?"

"Because I wanted it for myself!" said Hauser. "You don't understand how wonderful it was for me to be the only one in the world to have the Mozart cello concerto! That was worth more to me than all the money in the world! I would play it late at night when no one was around. But, one evening I was careless and Hess heard it when I thought he'd left the shop. I tried to make excuses that I was 'improvising' something, but that's when he got suspicious. And when the letter from Romano came and he saw it..."

"That's when he wrote to me," finished Stride.

"But why did you want to sell it at all?" asked Sam. He knew he should be quiet, but he was as intrigued as Stride and Kim about the fate of the manuscript.

"I am a sick man, and the doctors don't give me very long to live. If I had died with the manuscript in my possession, then my name would be forever dishonored. However, the man who was to purchase the manuscript from me would conceal the way he obtained it, so I would be in the clear."

"But why would you care about the money if. . . ?" Kim stopped mid-question.

Hauser paused, looking very tired. It was as if he were trying to figure out why he had done things the way he had. Finally, his voice straining to remain calm, he said, "It wasn't really about the money!" he exclaimed. "It was about knowing that I had the right manuscript. Anyway, the money was going to be given to a foundation in my memory, as a patron of the Mozarteum. If what I had done was discovered, they would never have accepted the donation. That title as patron would be my one piece of immortality."

"What are you going to do now?" asked Stride. Hauser quickly opened a desk drawer and pulled out a gun!

"What I've told you must never be repeated to a single soul. And that includes the three of you!" he said, pointing the gun at Stride.

"Really, Herr Hauser, you couldn't be capable of doing such a thing!" warned Stride.

"If I arranged the 'accident' to get rid of Abel Strauss, do you think at this time in my life I'd hesitate to keep the three of you quiet?" he asked, angrily.

"So, my vision was right!" said Kim.

"What vision? What is she talking about? Never mind. I'll report that I thought the three of you were intruders and fired before I realized who you were. The police would never suspect a harmless old man like me!"

"They do now!" said a voice from the other room. It was Karl Hess, and behind him were several policemen with their guns drawn. "Your game is finished, Hans. Drop that gun and no harm will come to you!"

With a mortified look on his face, Hauser dropped the gun and remained unresisting when a policeman approached him with handcuffs.

"I am grateful to you, Karl, for coming when you did and for bringing the police. How did you know to come here?" Stride asked his friend, embracing him.

"Lucky for you," said Hess, "I suspected that Hauser was up to something because he was acting so strangely, more secretive than usual, and I decided to watch his house. When I saw you and the children enter, I knew it was time to call the police."

"You arrived at exactly the right time. Now, let's pack these manuscripts into an envelope," said Stride.

The police officer informed Hauser that he was being charged for killing Abel Strauss and stealing the manuscript, as well as for threatening Professor Stride and the youngsters.

After watching the police take Hauser away, Stride saw both manuscripts on the table and asked the remaining detective, "Would it be alright if I take charge of these manuscripts, since I have been commissioned by my university to buy them? I will keep them locked in a vault for safe keeping until Hauser's trial. "

"I think that would be alright, Professor Stride. I know the whole story. Your friend Hess has filled me in," said the detective. "Please just sign this document which states that you are in possession of the manuscripts pending the date of the trial."

With that done, Stride, Kim and Sam brought the two manuscripts over to their residence by taxi. They didn't want to trust such a precious cargo by bike. When they had time to relax on the balcony, with the Untersberg in sight, they poured over the two manuscripts.

"Dad," asked Kim, "how can you tell which is the original and which is the copy?"

"Well, I look at the notation, for one thing, since I am well acquainted with Mozart's handwriting. Then, I look at changes made in notation. In the original, there will be more changes than in the copy. On the copy, the copier could just write out the corrections, not the errors. And, you know Mozart didn't make many changes; his music just came out in a pure form, no struggles like with Beethoven," Stride explained.

After looking at the two manuscripts carefully with a magnifying glass, he turned to Kim and Sam with a big smile on his face.

"I can already tell you that Hauser had the original manuscript after all. This is clearly a copy," said Stride pointing to the other one. "This other one is definitely Mozart's! There is a very characteristic way in which he forms his notes; you can see that the other is quite different, much neater." Carefully, he pointed out the differences between the notes on both manuscripts.

Then he said to Kim, "Would you like to touch it? It might give us more information if it has the same effect on you as the sculpture of the cellist. Just be very careful when you touch it; remember, it's over two hundred years old!"

While Kim was touching the manuscript, she had a sensation of needing to lie down. Something was happening to her, and she just had to go with the feeling. *She felt very light-headed and started seeing swirling lights, the kind of lights that had preceded her other visions. However, this was an even more powerful experience than any of the others. She closed her eyes, feeling tingling throughout her body. Then, a figure was taking shape, first the eyes, very sad eyes, were looking at her. Then, the shape of the head, that of an old man looking out a window with thick lines in front. She recognized these lines as bars! Was he in jail, or....the image became smaller as the background grew larger, until she could see a building made of gray and flat stone. Finally, she looked up over the door and saw the words, "Krankenhaus." Then she realized that the man looked familiar, or at least a younger version of him, from her earlier visions. Yes, that was the face of Abel Strauss! He must still be alive!*

CHAPTER THIRTEEN: KASPER

"Dad, he's alive, he's alive!" screamed Kim. "I just saw him. He's in a 'Krankenhaus.' What is that?"

"Kim, calm down. Who's alive?" asked Stride. "A Krankenhaus is a hospital. But, who is in a hospital?"

"I think that Kim will be in one if we don't calm her down," said Sam.

"Alright, let me tell you what I saw," said Kim. "There was the face of an old man with very sad eyes, and he was looking out of a window with bars. At first, I thought that it was a jail, except then I saw it was a very big building like in a park or something. There were trees all around it, so it couldn't be a jail. And, now you tell me it's a hospital. What kind of a hospital has bars on the windows?" asked Kim.

"Think again, Kimmy," said Sam. "It's obviously a mental hospital."

"That's right, Kim." said Stride, "But, who is it that you saw?"

"It was Abel Strauss! He's still alive," said Kim. "I guess he didn't die when he fell off that cliff. But, then why would he be in a mental hospital?"

"He must have lost his memory from the fall. Maybe he forgot who he was and someone just found him and brought him there," guessed Stride.

"Then, how do we find him? And, even more

importantly," said Sam, "how do we help him remember who he is?"

"With the manuscript," replied Kim. "Surely, he would remember the whole story if he saw the manuscript. After all, his father gave it to him, and Abel wanted to donate it to the conservatory. Dad, can we find that hospital? And, can we bring the original with us to show him?"

"Alright," said Stride. "Let's look up under the word Krankenhaus in the telephone book and see if there is one around here."

After looking up the address of a local mental hospital, they poured over a map to see where it was.

"I think that we will need a taxi for this trip," said Stride. "And, we will certainly bring the original manuscript as you suggested, Kim."

Finding the hospital was not hard, but finding Abel was much more difficult, since the clerk in the admissions office didn't have anyone there by that name.

"Well, what if we describe him," asked Kim. "Or better yet, maybe I can make a drawing of the face I saw in my vision." After she drew the picture of the man in her vision, the clerk immediately recognized him as someone they called Kasper. The doctor in charge, Dr. Klein, first interviewed them and told them that Kasper was found wandering around the bottom of the mountain a very long time ago after losing his memory. The person who found him took care of him for a while but then brought him there for longer-term care.

"Well, doctor," said Stride, "if this is the man we think he is, we may be able to help him regain his memory."

"Let me take you to him," Dr. Klein said, "and then we will see if this is actually the man you are looking for."

They went into a brightly-lit room that was located in the tower of the hospital, with nurses' stations in the middle of each wing. The place smelled slightly of cleaning fluid. Although quite spotless, it had a sterile atmosphere, as if nothing living was really supposed to be there.

"He's right in here," said Dr. Klein, who, despite his severe tone, had a kindly face. "I've been his physician for the past twenty years. He's quite harmless, you know, but he would never be able to survive in the outside world, not in his condition. Just talk very calmly. He doesn't get any visitors, and it might agitate him if you seemed excited. Besides, I very much doubt that 'Kasper' is the Abel Strauss you're looking for. This man has shown absolutely no interest in music, at least not when we've brought him to concerts at the Institute."

With those words, the doctor ushered Stride, Kim and Sam into a nice, bright room which consisted of a bed, some bookcases filled with detective novels and science fiction stories, and a white-haired, elderly gentleman, sitting and reading a book. He wore thick glasses and had the studious appearance of a life-long scholar.

"Hello, Kasper," said the doctor, gently. "You have some visitors. You don't know them, but they say they know something about you. Would you like to see them?"

The old man turned slowly and looked up. His face was expressionless, but he nodded and gave his hand for Stride, Kim and Sam to shake. Kim felt a strange kinship with this old man as she shook his hand, as if somehow they had something in common.

"It is a pleasure to meet you," he said, in a very soft voice. "I do not get visitors. What can I do for you?"

Dr. Klein quickly left with the warning, "Just be careful that you don't excite him. His health is quite frail."

"My name is Professor Daniel Stride. This is my daughter, Kim, and her friend, Sam," said Stride in German.

"You are American, are you not?" asked the old man in English. "You may speak with me in English. I do not have a chance to practice it, but I still can speak it."

"Mr. Kasper," began Kim, "have you ever heard of someone by the name of . . . Hans Hauser?"

There was a pause while the old man seemed to be trying to recall something. For a moment his face lit up, but then, it went back to being expressionless.

"I do not think I remember that name, but, of course, I don't remember very much of anything. Not even my own name!" He seemed to get agitated for a moment, but, with a deep breath, became calm again.

"Maybe we shouldn't press him now," said Stride. He was concerned about what the doctor said.

"Let me just try one thing more, Dad, please?" asked Kim.

"Well, what's that?" asked Stride.

"Show him the manuscript. Isn't that why you brought it?" she said.

"Well, I don't know, but. . . ." Before he had a chance to finish his thought, Kim impulsively took the manuscript from the envelope and placed it in Kasper's hands.

"*Was ist das?*" he muttered in German. "I mean, what is this you have given me?"

"It's something you lost, or rather, was stolen from you many years ago, at least, that's what we believe," said Stride.

The old man gingerly held the manuscript. Stride knew he was taking a chance, but he sensed that he had nothing to worry about as far as the safety of the manuscript was concerned.

"Do you read music?" asked Kim.

The old man stared at the first page of music for a long moment, his face in turn seeming to show a sign of recognition and then the blankness that was a sign of incomprehension.

"I do not know," he said, slowly. "But. . . ." He paused again and started to hum, in a thin, worn voice, the melody of the concerto. Suddenly, his eyes brightened!

"I remember! I remember!" he shouted. "The concerto, my father's precious manuscript! You have found it!"

His voice was loud enough for the doctor to hear him and come rushing in.

"What are you doing?" Dr. Klein asked Stride. "I told you not to upset him."

"No, no. That's all right, doctor. I am beginning to remember things," said the old man, still excited, but now more in control of himself.

"What do you remember, Kasper?" asked the doctor, gently.

"That I am not Kasper. I am . . . my name is Abel Strauss!"

CHAPTER FOURTEEN: A FAMILY REUNITED

After identifying Kasper as Abel Strauss, Stride, with help from Kim and Sam, was able to fill Abel in on everything that had happened to the manuscript since he fell off the Untersberg cliff and lost his memory. They were especially happy to tell him that Hauser was in jail awaiting trial.

"My main concern is that the manuscript is saved and can be given to the Mozarteum, just as I intended it in the first place," said Abel.

"And with the money from the sale of the copy, you can live quite well in Salzburg, or wherever you wish," said Stride.

"But, the copy is not mine," replied Abel, "I do not deserve any money for it."

"You need to live on something, and I think that it's only fair that you should get a share in the proceeds from the sale," replied Stride.

"Well, we shall see," said Abel. "In the meantime, I would like to present the Director of the Conservatory with the manuscript as soon as possible."

"We'll put the manuscript in the bank vault, and as soon as we make an appointment to see him, we will take it out," said Stride.

"There is one other matter," said Abel. "I now remember that I had a family—a dear father, mother and sister. Is there any way that I can find them?" he asked.

"Well, during the War, whole families were lost when the Nazis took over," said Stride, being careful not to say anything that would grieve this gentle old man. "Of course, we can try to find anyone who survived... who managed to come back to Germany or Austria."

"I would be so grateful if you would help me in this way. I can give you information, perhaps. I am beginning to recall the names of my family. There was my father, Aaron, my mother Greta and my sister Marta Strauss," said Abel.

"Did you say Greta?" asked Kim, remembering something her father said about her mother's grandmother's name.

"And did you say Marta?" asked Stride. "My late wife spoke of her mother's name as Marta Moser. But, there must be many women with the name Marta."

"But not many Marta Mosers," said Abel. "My sister, Marta, was being courted by a man named Gabriel Moser. He was not a Jew, but they were talking about getting married and going to America where they would not be discriminated against for Marta's Jewish background."

Kim, Stride and Sam were standing there, looking in amazement at Abel. He was just as amazed watching them. "Does that mean that...?" he started asking.

"We are related?" finished Kim, with growing excitement. "My mother's mother was Marta Moser, who was the daughter of Greta Strauss, which makes you...? My uncle?" she asked Abel.

"More like your grand uncle, Kim," said Stride, a big smile on his face. In fact, it was difficult for him to hold back tears of joy. "Now, I understand so much more. My wife, Gisella, used to treasure hearing Yiddish spoken, and I never knew that she was part Jewish and probably heard it at home from her mother. Her mother died when she was so young that she probably didn't remember where she heard it. Maybe her father didn't want to tell her about her Jewish background for fear of discrimination in the U.S."

"I felt something about you the first time I saw you in my vision," said Kim to Abel. "As if we were similar in some way, and now I find out that you are my grand uncle." Abel was crying tears of joy and opened his arms to embrace her.

Stride and Sam couldn't believe this turn of events. Suddenly, they found that they had family here in Salzburg. Kim was able to learn about her mother's heritage and found a dear grand uncle who was not only a musician, but someone with a gentle, loving nature.

In the next few days, they arranged to have Abel Strauss discharged from the "Krankenhaus," bringing him to the chalet with them. The next day, they decided to meet with Karl Hess at a café in town, where arrangements were made for donating the original manuscript to the Mozarteum.

The Director of the Mozarteum was overjoyed at the donation of the manuscript by Strauss and decided to hold a concert performance of the cello concerto in Strauss' honor. In addition, a lifetime stipend was awarded to Abel Strauss for his contribution to cover his expenses, wherever he chose to live.

Finally, the time had come for the concert in the

great hall of the Mozarteum. Seated next to Abel in the balcony were Professor Stride, Kim and Sam, as well as Karl Hess. After the orchestra tuned up, the conductor gave a standing ovation to Abel. The whole audience looked up and clapped.

The concert hall was especially festive this evening, with gleaming chandeliers, thick velvet curtains, and newly polished wooden doors. The cellist was the well-known favorite on the Mozarteum's faculty who also happened to be a woman.

Quite a change from the time of Mozart, thought Stride with a wry grin.

For the first time, Kim was able to hear the melody fully, having heard only parts of it in her visions.

During the intermission, Kim turned her head and saw, just behind the curtain in the last balcony, none other than the malicious Hans Hauser! She became very frightened.

"Dad, did Hauser get out of jail?"

"What do you mean, Kim?" asked Sam, also frightened.

"Oh, you can see him, can you?" asked Stride.

"You mean that you know he's here?" asked Kim, uncertainly.

"Don't worry," said Stride. "If you look closely, you'll see that he's wearing handcuffs. Abel Strauss, with enormous kindness, has allowed Hauser to come to this concert to hear the concerto. Hauser will be led away by a plainclothes policeman after the concert."

Finally, the time came to leave Salzburg. Kim and Sam were sad to go because now they had many new friends — Heidi, their landlady's daughter who would be their pen pal; Karl Hess, who had become their good friend, as well as Stride's friend; and of course, Abel Strauss who had been endearing from the first time they met him and now was Kim's newly-discovered grand uncle.

Abel had decided to live in Salzburg permanently, although he wanted to make a trip to Israel to visit. "I will go when there is peace there," he said. "I hope I may live to see such a day." And, he had invited the trio to visit him again next year. So, they looked forward to that.

They were still sad to leave Salzburg itself and all the wonderful memories — the bike rides through the meadows with distant church bells ringing the hours; the looming form of the Untersberg with the mist rising upwards in the mornings as they watched from the balcony; the Mozarteum with its jumble of sounds from musicians practicing and taking lessons; the old town of Salzburg with the Getreidegasse and all its little side streets leading into mysterious courtyards and hidden shops of music manuscripts. They took all these impressions of Salzburg with them.

On the plane ride home, there were a few loose ends they still didn't understand. Now, they had the time to sort them out.

"Dad, whatever happened to the money from the sale of the copy of the manuscript that you bought for the University?" asked Kim.

"Well, Kim, Mrs. Groschen was the owner of the copy, so she received the bulk of it, although she had to pay the dealer, Romano, his fee for finding a seller."

"But didn't they lie to you about the manuscript?" asked Sam.

"Yes, they did, but they were under instructions from Hauser, who wanted to sell the copy for more money than I was ready to pay. He also didn't want to part with the original. There was mention of some

American industrialist who was ready to pay him four million dollars for the original. Yes, we were certainly sent on a wild goose chase," said Stride. "But, I didn't make an issue of that, so the whole case about their complicity was dropped."

"Gosh, Dad, you were just as kind to these losers as Abel," said Kim.

"Well, actually, Abel was the kindest of all. After all, Hauser tried to kill him and stole his manuscript, but Abel asked the police to go easy on him and even had a cello brought to him in his cell," said Stride.

"You know what, Dad?" said Kim. "I think I want to learn to play the cello!"

"Oh, I think that can be arranged," said Stride.

"Me, too," said Sam. "After all, I don't want to be left out of this."

Finally, the plane landed, and they made their way back to their own little college town. Sam's mother was there to greet them.

"Welcome home, Sam," she said. "Did you have a pleasant time?"

"Oh, mom, you wouldn't believe the time we had!" exclaimed Sam.

"And, how about you, Kim? Did you continue to have any of those out-of-time experiences?" she asked.

"I had my share of those experiences, enough to last a very long time, Mrs. Berlow," replied Kim. "They're not so confusing anymore. In fact, I am beginning to feel comfortable with them."

Once they were home, Kim and Sam went back to school and talked about their adventures in Salzburg, Vienna, Venice, and the Alps of Switzerland.

As at the beginning of their adventure, Kim and Sam found themselves again walking past the little white dog on their walks. And, once again, the dog started barking at Kim and Sam as they passed its house. This time, however, Kim said, "Sam, I want you to think loving thoughts and send them to this little dog."

"Oh, you've got to be kidding, Kim," said Sam.

"No, I mean it, Sam. Just try," said Kim with a quiet confidence.

"Oh, alright, but I don't think I have your talent," said Sam, not believing he could do it. But, he did try. He concentrated all his attention on sending loving thoughts to the little dog, even feeling kindly towards this cute, fluffy pup, seeing beyond its meanness.

Strangely enough, the little dog looked rather doubtful of his own viciousness and stopped barking. It just stood there, looking blankly befuddled as the two experienced travelers passed by.

ABOUT THE AUTHOR

Joanne grew up in Brooklyn, New York. She studied music at the High School of Music and Art and majored in Music, English and Comparative Literature at Queens College, CUNY. She took many trips to Salzburg, Austria, where she studied piano and received a teaching diploma in Orff music and movement for children at the Mozarteum. Eventually, she earned a Ph.D. in English from the University of Massachusetts in Amherst and taught English literature and written composition at numerous universities in the United States and abroad. She now lives in Durham, North Carolina, and works as a volunteer group leader for International House at Duke University. Ten years after its first publication, this book is reprinted as an offering to the book club for international spouses, which she leads. She recently received recognition as an international educator from International House. Joanne also enjoys reading, playing piano in chamber groups, folk dancing, writing poetry and stories, watercolor painting, and taking long walks accompanying her husband and two dogs.

Made in the USA
Columbia, SC
16 June 2020